mary-kate olsen    ashley olsen

# so little time

## spring breakup

By Emma Harrison

Based on the series Created by Eric Cohen
and Tonya Hurley

HarperEntertainment
An Imprint of HarperCollinsPublishers

A PARACHUTE PRESS BOOK

## A PARACHUTE PRESS BOOK

Parachute Publishing, L.L.C.
156 Fifth Avenue, Suite 302
New York, NY 10010

Published by
HarperEntertainment

An *Imprint of* HarperCollins*Publishers*
10 East 53rd Street, New York, NY 10022-5299

ISBN 0-06-059069-6

HarperCollins®, ☂®, and HarperEntertainment™ are trademarks of HarperCollins Publishers Inc.

First printing: March 2004

Printed in the United States of America

Visit HarperEntertainment on the World Wide Web at
www.harpercollins.com

10 9 8 7 6 5 4 3 2 1

# chapter one

"**J**ust think. Twenty-four hours from now we will officially be on spring break!" Chloe Carlson announced.

"And forty-eight hours from now we might be partying with Jonah Bayou," her twin sister, Riley, put in.

"Okay, you guys have thirty seconds to stop being so excited," Riley's best friend, Sierra, said, slouching in her seat at the Newsstand, their favorite coffee bar. "I can't believe I'm going to miss out on the *Teen Scene* Beach House to go on an educational tour of Colonial Williamsburg with the 'rents. This is going to be the worst-ever spring break."

"Your mom and dad *need* to join us in the twenty-first century," Riley told her friend with a sympathetic sigh.

Chloe felt sorry for Sierra with her worst-ever spring break plans. But at the moment that wasn't enough to bring Chloe down. She was just too psyched. *Teen Scene* was the coolest music show on television, and it was bringing its annual Spring Break Beach House right here to West Malibu. It was going to be seven days of dancing in the sun, chilling with celebrities, and maybe even getting her face on television. Plus Jonah Bayou, the totally hot host of the show, was going to be there all week, running the party. It was a dream come true. It wasn't fair that Sierra couldn't be there with them.

"We'll get you Jonah's autograph and tell you every detail," Chloe promised.

Sierra forced a smile. "Thanks," she said.

Quinn Reyes, Tara Jordan, and Amanda Gray—three more of Chloe's closest friends—came up to the table, carrying iced coffees.

"So, have you guys figured out the fashion plan yet?" Quinn asked, pulling her chair in close.

"High-heeled sandals or flip-flops? That is the question," Chloe said.

"Heels, definitely," Tara said, sipping from her straw. "They're much more flattering."

"But harder to dance in," Riley pointed out.

"And flip-flops are casual chic. That's totally in," Quinn added.

"Well, our shoes aren't going to matter if we don't get into the House," Amanda said in her usual quiet voice. "I read in *Flair* that they turned a thousand people away last year when the House was in San Diego."

"We're going to get in," Chloe said, confidently tossing her wavy, dark-blond hair over her shoulder. "All we have to do is impress the *Teen Scene* people with our dazzling looks and our sparkling personalities."

"No problem there," a familiar voice said.

Chloe looked up to find her boyfriend, Lennon Porter, coming toward them, smiling his sweet smile. She couldn't help smiling right back. Just seeing Lennon made her happy.

"Everyone, this is Seth Rovino," Lennon said, introducing the guy next to him.

"Hey," Seth said, lifting a hand. He was tall with reddish-blond hair, a deep tan, and a smattering of cute freckles.

"Hey! You're in my English class, right?" Riley asked.

"Yeah," Seth said, snagging the chair next to Riley's. "That last poem you wrote was killer. I was going to ask you if you wanted to submit it to the literary magazine."

"Really? You're on the staff?" Riley asked.

"I'm one of the editors," Seth said.

"Cool," Riley said, clearly impressed.

"Okay, people. Let's get back to the important stuff," Chloe suggested. "Bikinis or tankinis? Pros and cons?"

Lennon and Seth both laughed. "Sounds like we stumbled in on an important debate," Lennon joked.

"It's *way* important," Tara told him. "It could decide whether or not we get to meet Jonah Bayou."

"You guys are doing the *Teen Scene* thing? That's cool," Seth said.

"You should come," Riley suggested. "It's going to be totally amazing."

"We're all going down there early on Saturday morning," Chloe put in. "I want to be first on line."

"I'm there," Lennon said.

"I can't make it Saturday. I have a basketball game," Seth said. "But maybe later in the week."

"Okay, but just remember, fashion is key," Chloe warned him. "The *Teen Scene* people are very picky. They'll only let in the coolest of the cool."

At that moment Larry Slotnick, Chloe and Riley's crazy neighbor and classmate, burst into the Newsstand wearing a loud Hawaiian shirt, wraparound sunglasses, and a huge straw hat.

"I'm ready for my close-up, baby!" he said, throwing his arms wide.

Chloe caught Riley's eye and frowned. W*hat* was Larry *thinking*?

"You're going to wear *that* to *Teen Scene*?" Quinn asked in her direct way.

Larry looked worried—but only for a second. "It's the hat, isn't it?" he asked. "No problem. I have an alternate."

He whipped a crushed fisherman's hat from his back pocket and replaced the straw one with it.

"Well?" he said, grinning and turning his head from side to side. "Do you love it?"

Chloe realized that if Larry was going to come along

with them, she was going to have to give him a crash course in fashion. Otherwise they'd *never* get into the House.

"Larry, this outfit is definitely . . . original," Chloe said, walking over to him. "But what if we lose the hat?" She took it off and tossed it to Quinn.

"And maybe untuck the shirt," Riley added, getting up and pulling the hem of the Hawaiian shirt from Larry's shorts.

"And you're going to need some new shades," Chloe added, stealing Larry's reflectors right off his face. "There. Much better."

"Thanks, girls, but I think I can dress myself," Larry said. He rolled his eyes, as if Chloe and Riley's suggestions were just *so* ridiculous, then gathered his stuff and strode out.

"He was kidding, right?" Chloe said.

Riley shrugged. "With Larry you just never know."

"Maybe we should go to his house Saturday morning and dress him ourselves," Chloe said.

She looked at Riley, and they both cracked up laughing. Not even *Teen Scene* was worth seeing Larry Slotnick in his underwear.

We're just going to have to hope for the best, Chloe thought.


"That was Rocketship with 'Love in the Stars,' one of my least favorite songs in the world," Charlie Slater said into the microphone at the West Malibu High radio studio on Friday morning.

"But we played it anyway because I love it," Riley added, speaking into her own mike.

"Now here's some actual music," Charlie said as he cued up the next song. "It's 'Rage On' by Sick Cylinder. Listen up!"

Charlie hit the button to mute their microphones and start the song.

Riley laughed. "Think we're ever going to agree on any song?" she asked.

"Not a chance," Charlie replied, leaning back in his chair with a smile. "Unless you develop some taste, that is. I keep hoping that since I'm such a good influence—"

"You are so deluded!" Riley said, swatting him with a playlist, but she was grinning as she said it.

Riley and Charlie had been butting heads ever since they started working together at the radio station. They were co-DJs on the school's *Morning Death Rant* show. At first Charlie had annoyed her. But after awhile Riley realized that in addition to being a pain, Charlie was smart and interesting and funny.

[Riley: Okay, at first he drove me straight up the wall. Not only did Charlie insist on that dumb name for the show, but he also played the worst music *and* he had the nerve to dis the bands I liked. Actually, none of that has changed. We're still total opposites. But when I quit the station (temporarily), I realized I missed Charlie. Even weirder, Charlie missed me. Go figure.]

To Riley's amazement, their show was a hit, and she and her co-DJ had each admitted that they liked the other. Now all they had to do was go out on their first date.

Riley felt a little thrill of excitement as she looked at Charlie. With spring break about to start, there was a whole week full of opportunities for them to get together.

"So, any big plans for spring break yet?" Charlie asked, as if reading her mind.

Riley flushed slightly. Could Charlie be asking because *he* was interested in making plans with her? She hoped so.

"Actually, my friends and I are all going down to the *Teen Scene* Beach House tomorrow," she said. "You should come."

Charlie laughed. "I don't think so. Not my style."

"Why am I not surprised?" Riley asked. "Are you allergic to fun?"

"No. I like fun. But all that wholesome, perfect-for-TV stuff? *Teen Scene* is not fun," Charlie replied.

[Riley: I could have told you he'd say something like that. Practically the moment we met, Charlie accused me of being too mainstream. Then he hit me with what was, for him, the worst insult of all: He said I was a "cheerleader-type." I guess he's kind of allergic to anything that isn't alternative.]

"Okay, so what are *you* doing tomorrow?" Riley asked.

"Actually, I promised my dad I'd help him at work," Charlie said.

"Oh, *that's* fun," Riley joked.

"Well, it is, usually. He runs this underground record store called Fracture," Charlie said. "Ever heard of it?"

"Nope."

"Why am I not surprised?" Charlie teased.

Riley rolled her eyes and laughed.

"Anyway, business has been down and I told him I'd help him figure out some ways to bring in customers," Charlie added.

"I have an idea," Riley said. "How about you give the Beach House a try, and I'll help you come up with ideas for Fracture?"

Charlie looked doubtful. "I don't know if that's an even trade."

"Fine. Turn me down. But you'll be missing out on one of the most brilliant creative minds of West Malibu High," Riley said, shrugging casually.

Charlie grinned. "Well, when you put it that way . . ."

"Besides, I'd love for you to hang out with my sister and our friends," Riley admitted.

"Okay, I'll come," Charlie said. "But then you have to hang out with me and some of *my* friends on Saturday night."

Riley's heart skipped a beat. Charlie wanted her to meet his friends. And he was going to hang with hers. Could this be getting serious?

It was way too soon to tell, but the idea made Riley smile.

"It's a deal," she told him.

Riley felt a little shiver of happiness. This was going to be the *best*-ever spring break!

# chapter
## two

**"I** cannot believe how many people are here," Chloe said.

She bit her lip as she attempted to count the kids ahead of her on line. It was pointless. The *Teen Scene* Beach House was mobbed. Girls in bikini tops and denim shorts chatted with guys in board shorts and Ray-Bans. The crowd was so intense that a guy had set up a cart across the street selling sodas and ices.

"This is as bad as trying to get tickets for a Rocket-ship concert." Tara moaned.

"Worse," Amanda said. "Because everyone here is totally nervous. All anyone's talking about is who will be cool enough to get in and who won't."

Chloe noticed that Riley was standing on tiptoe, craning her neck to see over the crowd. "Who are you looking for?" Chloe asked.

"Charlie. I told him to meet us here, but I don't

know how he'll ever find us in this mess," Riley replied.

"Wait a minute. Charlie Slater? You invited the most antisocial guy in the entire school to the Beach House?" Tara asked.

Riley laughed. "He's not *that* bad."

"Are you sure he's coming?" Chloe asked. "I mean, he doesn't exactly seem like the fun-in-the-sun type. Not that there's anything wrong with that," she added quickly.

[Chloe: Okay, I know that Riley has a crush on Charlie. I'm just not sure why. I mean, he's cute and all, but he's definitely not the type of guy Riley usually dates—or even talks to. But, hey! Maybe it's a good thing he's coming today. Now I can get to know him and hopefully see what Riley sees under all that scruffy hair and those black punk T-shirts.]

"I'm sure he'll have fun once he gets here," Riley said.

"Oh, look!" Quinn said, going up on tiptoe. "They're letting people in."

Chloe's heart gave an excited flutter. "Okay, now remember, look cool!"

"Cool, right, that's us," Lennon said in a serious voice.

Riley tossed her hair behind her shoulders and gazed into the distance, as if she were posing for a portrait. Quinn and Tara both put on bored-fashion-model expressions, as if they got invited into the Beach House every day. Lennon and Amanda looked perfectly relaxed. So why did Chloe feel as if she were about to have a heart attack?

Please let us get in, she thought as a guy with a clipboard walked down the line. If we get in, I'll never put the empty FroYo container back into the freezer again.

"Hey! Sorry I'm late, everyone! But never fear, Larry is here!" Larry wrapped his arms around Chloe and Riley and pulled them into a hug. When he let them go, Chloe took a step back, looked him over, and winced.

It was even worse than she'd expected. Larry was wearing an outfit that could have been ripped from the *Beverly Hills 90210* set—in the early years. He had on a bright pink button-down shirt, black-and-pink striped pants, hightops, and a *Teen Scene* baseball cap. Everyone knew you didn't wear the logo of the show you were trying to impress. It was just *so* not cool.

"Can you say 'trying too hard'?" Riley whispered to Chloe.

Over Larry's shoulder Chloe saw the casting guy getting closer and closer. She had to think fast. They could not be seen with Larry, or their chances of spending spring break at the *Teen Scene* Beach House were toast.

"Larry! It's great you're here," Chloe said, grabbing his arm. "But I am *so* thirsty. Would you mind getting us some sodas from that cart over there?"

"Sure," Larry said, glancing over his shoulder. "Anybody else want something to drink?"

"I do!" Riley, Tara, Quinn, and Amanda all joined in, catching on to the plan.

Tara handed Larry some money and turned him toward the cart. "Take your time," she said.

Larry started toward the cart, and Chloe sighed with relief. Until she saw the casting guy heading her way.

"Okay, you two go in," the casting guy said to a pair of girls right in front of Chloe. She saw him hand them two laminated passes with the *Teen Scene* logo on them. So cool.

"Here he comes," Chloe said under her breath.

Riley gave Chloe's hand a quick squeeze. Chloe knew her sister was every bit as excited as she was. This was it, the chance they'd been waiting for, one of the most amazing opportunities ever.

The casting director walked up to them, looked them over from beneath his shades . . . and kept walking.

"He did not just pass us by," Chloe said, her heart falling.

"I think he kind of did," Lennon said.

Chloe could not believe it. They had all worn their coolest clothes. She had spent an entire hour in front of the mirror making sure her hair and makeup and clothes were perfect. She'd even double-checked that each eyelash was properly curled! This was not acceptable.

"We have to do something," she said, determined.

"Like what? We don't have passes," Riley told her.

Chloe saw a big guy unloading electrical equipment from a truck behind the house. He was taking the equipment in through a back door just barely visible from where she was standing. There was no time to double-think it.

"See that door?" she said to her friends, narrowing her eyes. "We're going in." She led them away from the line and over to the truck.

"Wait! Chloe!" Riley rushed up to her. "We can't go in without Charlie."

"This is our only chance," Chloe replied. She lifted a huge light from the truck and struggled with it until Lennon took it from her with one hand.

"What are you doing?" Riley said in an undertone. "We don't know anything about lighting."

"Do you want to get into the *Teen Scene* Beach House or not?" Chloe asked.

"Hey, Riley!"

Chloe and Riley looked up to see Charlie jogging over to them, shouting Riley's name. Everyone on line looked over—including the casting director.

"Where are you guys going?" Charlie asked, catching up to them.

Chloe saw the casting director stalking their way. He did not look happy.

"Nowhere, now," she said sadly.

"What do you kids think you're doing?" the casting director demanded.

"Well, we were just . . . trying to be helpful!" Chloe said with a huge grin, gesturing to Lennon. He held up the light to illustrate, but she knew it wasn't going to help. They were snagged.

"Hey! Sodas all around!"

Larry appeared next to the casting director. Like a waiter, he was holding the five huge cups of soda pressed together between his hands. He paused when he saw them all standing near the back door, and his face fell.

"Were you guys going in without me?" he asked.

"No! We just—" Chloe began.

"Oh, that's great. Send Larry off for sodas and then try to ditch him." Larry was getting all worked up.

Chloe saw a couple of the sodas start to slip. Then everything seemed to happen in slow motion. Larry lost his grip, fumbled with the filled-to-the-brim cups, and dumped them all over the white shirt of the one man who might still be able to get them into the Beach House.

Tara and Quinn screeched and jumped out of the way. Amanda, Riley, and Lennon winced. Charlie laughed. The casting director was dripping with sticky, syrupy liquid.

Chloe lifted her shoulders. "Any chance you found that refreshing?" she asked, hoping for a laugh.

The casting director's face turned purple. "All of you!" he shouted. "Get out!"

Riley leaned back against the bamboo fence that surrounded the *Teen Scene* Beach House. Inside, the music was pumping and every so often someone would screech or laugh or shout someone's name. It sounded like the party of the year.

"We have to get in there," Riley said, looking at Chloe and the rest of their friends.

"I don't see what the big deal is," Charlie said. "Why do you want to hang out at a place that's so totally superficial anyway?"

"Superficial? This is *Teen Scene*!" Quinn said. "It's the coolest show on TV."

"Well, apparently they didn't think you guys were cool enough to get in," Charlie said. "I mean, doesn't that bother you? Why do you want to party with a bunch of snobs?"

"Look, there's no reason to argue," Riley said, stepping between them. "We just have to think. Are there any other ways to get ourselves passes?"

Just then a huge stretch limo pulled up near the back door of the house. A big guy in a black T-shirt and black pants stepped out. He looked around, then reached in to help someone else from the car. A beautiful blonde in a pink halter top and perfectly snug, hip-slung jeans stepped out of the limo. Riley couldn't believe her eyes.

"Omigosh. It's Nariah," Chloe said, grabbing Riley's hand.

"I heard she's doing a concert this Friday at the arena," Amanda said.

"I heard she's dating Jonah Bayou," Quinn put in.

"I heard they're engaged," Riley added.

"I heard they already got married in Hawaii and there's a bidding war for the pictures," Tara said.

Nariah was the hottest pop singer of the moment. Her newest CD, *You Know You Love Me*, had debuted at number one the week before. Riley watched as two more cars pulled up and a bunch of stylish people crowded around Nariah. Together they all started for the back door of the Beach House.

"This is it, you guys," Riley said. "This is our chance."

"Huh?" Charlie said.

"Look at all those people!" Riley said. "We can slip inside with them. Just try to blend in."

Riley and Chloe and their friends moved away from the bamboo fence. One by one they drifted toward Nariah's entourage. There were so many people clustered around the singer, no one noticed when a few more joined the crowd. Riley was impressed that all her friends were able to look so calm and collected in the presence of a superstar. Even Charlie looked like he didn't care.

**[Riley: That's probably because he doesn't. Charlie's so into punk, I don't think he's even heard of Nariah!]**

17

"This is going to work," Chloe whispered as the back door opened. "Riley, you're a genius."

"Hey, baby, how you doin'?" Larry said, pointing at one of Nariah's backup singers. "Yeah. I got my Hummer parked out of the sun. Gotta protect the paint job, know what I mean?"

"Larry!" Riley said through her teeth. "What are you doing?"

"Blending," Larry said. "Don't worry. I speak the lingo." He looked up at the enormous bouncer as they walked in. "Hey, bud. Keep an eye on my ride, would ya?" Before Riley could reach out and grab his arm, Larry flipped the guy a quarter.

The bouncer glanced at the coin, clearly confused, then stepped in front of them.

"Hold up," he said, stretching out his beefy arms. "Nariah! These kids with you?"

Nariah turned around, lowered her trendy sunglasses, and looked Riley and her friends up and down. Riley still couldn't believe the superstar was standing three feet away. She tried to send her a psychic message: *We're huge fans. We buy all your CDs. Help us get in! Please!*

"Nope. Never seen them before," Nariah said. Then she turned and strode off with her friends.

**[Riley: So I won't be working at the Psychic Hotline anytime soon.]**

"All right, kids. Nice try," the bouncer told them, crowding them back out the door.

Riley couldn't even bring herself to look at Charlie. This was too depressing.

"Hey, Ronnie! Hang on a sec!" someone shouted.

A tall, handsome, older guy walked toward them. He was wearing a black T-shirt and black pants, like the other bouncer. "Larry?" he said.

Larry's face lit up. "Cousin Barty?"

The two guys hugged and slapped each other's backs.

"Dude! What are you *wearing*?" Barty asked when he pulled away.

"You like?" Larry asked, executing a little turn.

"It's definitely you," Barty said. "Come on, cuz. I'll introduce you to Jonah."

Riley and Chloe looked at each other and mouthed a *Yes!* They were in! All thanks to Larry and his gorgeous cousin.

They started after Larry and Barty with the rest of their friends, but Ronnie held out his arms again.

"Oh, no," he said. "Not you. Just him."

Riley's mouth dropped open. "Larry, wait!" she called after him.

[Riley: I know what you're thinking. Larry may be strange, but he's always been a good friend. He wouldn't really shut us out of our dream spring break, would he? Think again.]

19

Larry paused and turned around. For a second Riley thought they were saved, but then he gave them an I'm-too-cool smile and waved.

Then he and Barty disappeared around the corner, and Ronnie closed the door right in Riley's face.

# chapter
## three

"How could Larry do this to us?" Chloe wailed.

"Um . . . we tried to do it to him," Lennon pointed out.

"Let's just leave," Riley said. "It's too depressing hanging out here, listening to all the fun inside."

Chloe didn't want to give up yet, but she was out of ideas. Feeling glum, she led her friends around the back of the Beach House toward the boardwalk. The other kids who had been turned away were also starting to give it up and go home. Everyone looked as crushed as Chloe felt.

"Well, let's look on the bright side," Amanda said, attempting to smile. "At least we're still on spring break."

"Yeah," Chloe added, brightening a bit. "We still have nine whole days to do whatever we want."

"While everyone else we know dances with Jonah Bayou," Quinn added, refusing to be cheered.

"Including Larry Slotnick," Tara said, glumly.

Chloe frowned. This was *so* lame. Not to mention unfair.

"Hey! Where do you guys think you're going?" Larry called out.

Chloe stopped in her tracks and turned around slowly. She didn't dare believe what she was seeing. Was it just her wishful thinking, or was Larry Slotnick really standing at the side door with a bunch of passes dangling from one fist?

"Larry! How did you get those?" Riley asked, starting toward him.

Larry shrugged casually as he handed out the passes. He slipped one over Chloe's head and grinned. "I have my ways," he said, like he was Mr. Cool.

At that moment, to Chloe he *was* the coolest guy on the planet. She gave him a giddy kiss on the cheek and smiled.

"Larry, I swear I will never try to ditch you again!" she promised. Then she grabbed Riley's hand and pulled her into the *Teen Scene* Beach House. It was time to party!

"All right, everyone, I'd like to welcome you to the *Teen Scene* Spring Break Beach House!" Jonah Bayou shouted into his microphone. Everyone gathered around the huge pool and screamed and clapped. Chloe was so giddy, she could have floated into the air with the balloons that dotted the bamboo fence. It was really Jonah Bayou. Jonah Bayou was standing on a stage twenty feet away from her!

> [Chloe: Okay, I love Lennon and all. But Jonah Bayou? Hello? Those big blue eyes. That thick brown hair. And the dimples! Can you say swoon-worthy?]

"Now I want everyone to get your groove on, 'cause the cameras are rolling. And if you impress us, you just might find yourself on the *Teen Scene* 'Spring Break Special'!" Jonah announced to another roar of applause. "So let's get the party started with Nariah!"

Nariah came out from backstage and launched into her latest single, "The Beat of My Heart." Chloe, Riley, and their friends danced up a storm. More than once Chloe caught a camera trained on her and her friends for a good couple of minutes.

"We're going to be on *Teen Scene*. I know it!" Chloe said.

"You bet!" Lennon replied with a grin.

"This is so cool!" Riley added. "I just wish Charlie would dance with us," she said, glancing over at the snack bar.

Chloe followed her sister's gaze and saw Charlie watching the dancers with an amused sort of smirk on his face. Something about the way he was looking at everyone bothered Chloe. It was like he thought they were all so uncool or something.

"I thought you said he was going to have fun once he got here," Chloe said.

"Well, he *is* smiling," Riley replied.

After a couple of songs Nariah took a break, and Riley grabbed Chloe's hand. "Let's go get something to drink. I'm totally parched," Riley said.

Chloe reluctantly followed Riley toward the snack bar. She had just seen one of the cameras swooping toward them as they danced. She'd been sure it was going to get a good shot of her and her sister. Oh, well. They had all week for that.

"Hey!" Riley said to Charlie as she climbed up onto the stool next to his. "Were you planning on getting off your butt anytime today?"

"Nah. I'm too amused by the people-watching," Charlie said.

"What do you mean?" Chloe asked.

"I've never seen more lame dancing," Charlie said. "Of course, it's not your fault. It's the music that stinks."

Chloe's mouth fell open, she was so offended. She was about to say something, but Riley beat her to it.

"So you're saying *we* look bad out there?" Riley asked.

To Chloe she didn't sound angry at all.

[Chloe: You're probably wondering what I was going to say. I have no idea. But it would have put Mr. I'm-Too-Cool-to-Dance in his place. At least more than Riley's unsnappy comeback did.]

"Like I said, it's not your fault," Charlie replied.

Riley laughed, which surprised Chloe. Shouldn't she have been defending their moves *and* one of their favorite singers?

"I'd like to see you do better," Riley challenged him.

"Give me some real music and I will," Charlie shot back.

Chloe looked up at the guy working the snack bar. "Two waters, please," she said, choosing not to get sucked into a conversation she didn't quite understand.

"Well, we're having fun out there, right, Chloe?" Riley asked.

"Absolutely. And it's gotta be better than sitting over here all day," Chloe said. "You really should join us," she told Charlie.

"Nah. I have a better view of the stage from here. I've already seen Nariah mess up her lip-syncing three times. Plus I caught that loser, Jonah Bayou, checking out his hair for fifteen minutes in that mirror back there," Charlie said. "What a pretty-boy."

Chloe looked up, and sure enough, there was a par- tially open door behind the stage that led to a dressing room. Jonah was fixing his hair with some kind of gel and patting it down.

"Well, he's on TV. He has to look good," Chloe said.

"No guy should spend that much time with his reflection," Charlie said.

"Well, maybe if you bothered to look in a mirror once in a while, you wouldn't always have that hair sticking up at the back of your head," Riley teased.

Charlie blushed slightly, reached up, and patted his hair.

Chloe got the sense that her sister had just scored some kind of victory, but she wasn't sure. She just did not get the way Riley and Charlie talked with one another. They didn't act like they were thinking about dating. They acted more like they were brother and sister.

**[Chloe: Ick.]**

"Hey, you girls and guys want to come up onstage for a spotlight dance?" Jonah Bayou asked from the stage just to Chloe's left.

Chloe instantly went mute. Jonah Bayou was talking to her! But Quinn, Tara, and Amanda, who had just joined them from the dance floor, squealed with excitement.

"Let's go, you guys!" Tara said, grabbing hold of Chloe's arm.

Chloe stood up, her knees shaking with nervousness.

Lennon grasped her other arm. It took her a moment to realize that Riley wasn't coming with them.

"Riley! It's a spotlight dance!" Chloe said as she climbed the stairs to the stage. "We'll *definitely* make the 'Spring Break Special'!"

Riley laughed and waved Chloe on. "You guys go without me. I'm going to hang here for a while."

Chloe was so surprised, she almost tripped over the last step. But luckily she managed to steady herself before she hit the stage. She couldn't believe Riley was passing up the opportunity to dance on TV with her. Had Charlie hypnotized her or something?

"Okay, everyone. Just stay in the middle of the stage and do your thang!" Jonah Bayou told them.

He pointed at the DJ at the end of the stage, and a pounding dance tune filled the air.

Chloe moved to the music with her friends, smiling and trying to get into the spirit, but every once in a while she couldn't help looking over at her sister. Riley was laughing and flirting with Charlie. She looked like she was having the time of her life. Chloe didn't get it.

How could Riley want to chat with Charlie-the-Boring instead of dancing in front of the cameras with us? she wondered as the lens swooped in close to her face.

Chloe caught herself and grinned for the camera, but even though she was having fun, she couldn't help

27

feeling something was off. Here was this incredible opportunity to appear on the hottest show on TV. Riley should have been in that shot with her, but she wasn't, thanks to Charlie. Chloe had a sudden, sinking feeling that Riley's new guy was going to ruin their spring break.

# chapter four

Riley flushed as Charlie slipped his arms around her. Just a few dozen yards away the waves were crashing onto the shore. It would have been a totally romantic evening, except he was only holding her to show her how to keep her balance on a skateboard.

"Okay, hold your arms out like that," Charlie said, stepping away. "Perfect! Now kick off with your right foot."

Riley did as instructed and rolled over the smooth asphalt surface of the skate park. She smiled as she skimmed across the course, taking a loop with a few easy hills. She had only skateboarded a couple of times before, but thanks to her killer surfing skills and Charlie's help, keeping her balance was no problem. Skateboarding was turning out to be a piece of cake.

"Nice job!" Charlie applauded.

"Thank you very much," Riley said. She brought her

toe down on the edge of the board, popped it up, and caught it. "I've always wanted to do that," she said.

"Lookin' good," Charlie said. "But before you turn pro on me, maybe we should go over a few tricks."

For the next half hour Charlie taught Riley some basic boarding moves. First she learned to turn and stop without falling. Then she made it through a few small jumps. Charlie was impressed with her progress and Riley was pretty proud of herself, too.

Watch out, Tony Hawk! she thought as she made her highest jump and landed safely.

"The guys are gonna lose it when they see how good you are," Charlie told her as she skidded to a stop. "I told them we'd meet them up on the boardwalk. Want to get some ice cream?"

"I've never said no to a good twist cone," Riley said.

Together they walked to Swirly's, the best ice cream stand on the boardwalk.

"Can I help you?" the girl behind the counter asked.

Charlie stepped aside so that Riley could order first.

"I'd like a swirl cone with rainbow sprinkles, please," she said.

Charlie ordered a chocolate-dipped cone, then paid for both while Riley was still fishing for her wallet. She had to smile at his gentlemanly behavior.

[Riley: I'm all for girl power, but you've got to love it when a guy is so thoughtful. Sometimes I think that all guys have on their minds is video-game

strategies, baseball stats, and wondering whether
or not they're going to get to kiss you at the end
of the date. Okay, I guess I think about that last
one a lot, too!]

"Let's sit on the edge of the boardwalk," Riley suggested.

The sun was about to go down, and she loved watching it sink into the waves.

They sat side by side, close together but not quite touching. A line of high, thin clouds blazed orange-red against a deep blue sky.

"Don't tell anyone, but this is the best show in town," Charlie said. "It's never the same, it's always amazing, and it's free."

"It is pretty awesome," Riley agreed. Inside, though, she was thinking that if Chloe heard that, she'd understand why Riley liked Charlie. "So." Riley ate some more of her ice cream. "When do you think your friends will get here?"

Charlie checked his watch. "They should be here any minute."

"I hope they don't think I'm a total klutz on the board," Riley said.

"You look great," Charlie said, making Riley's heart flutter. "I mean, out there. You look great out there on the skateboard," he added, blushing slightly. "Okay, actually, you look great now, too."

Now it was Riley's turn to flush. Before she knew

what was happening, Charlie was leaning in toward her. Riley moved her ice cream cone away at the last second and closed her eyes. A moment later Charlie's chocolate-sweetened lips touched hers. As the sun sank into the ocean and her ice cream started to melt onto her hand, Riley had her first kiss with Charlie.

"Mmm," Charlie said. "That was good but not perfect."

Riley's eyes flew open. "What do you mean?" she asked indignantly. Were they even going to disagree about kissing? "I thought that was pretty terrific."

"Well, yeah," Charlie said. He was grinning now. "But maybe we'd better try it again, see if we can get it right."

"Oh," Riley said, smiling back at him. "Yeah, maybe we'd better."

Riley closed her eyes, and they kissed again.

This time it was *definitely* perfect.

"Smoochy, smoochy, smoochy!" a voice called out, causing Riley and Charlie to spring apart.

"Don't stop because of us, dude!"

A pair of scruffy-looking guys holding skateboards walked toward Riley and Charlie. The guy on the right was tall with blond hair and a tattoo of a dragon that ran up his neck and onto his left cheek. The guy on the left was short with multiple ear-piercings and brown hair that hung over his face. For a second Riley was slightly scared, until Charlie stood up and slapped hands with each of them.

"Riley, this is Jesse and Frodo," Charlie said as Riley scrambled to her feet.

"She's cute," Jesse, the one with the tattoo, said bluntly.

Riley blinked. Who said stuff like that right to a person's face?

"Nice to meet you," Frodo put in.

"You, too," Riley said, managing a smile. She wondered if Frodo was his real name. He certainly did resemble a hobbit.

"You guys wanna head back down to the skate park?" Charlie asked.

"You sure your girl's up to it?" Jesse asked. "She looks a little *girly* to me."

"I can hold my own," Riley shot back, discarding the rest of her ice cream in a nearby garbage can. These guys obviously didn't think she could board, but she would show them.

"Well, let's see then," Jesse challenged.

Five minutes later Riley was speeding around the skate park, grinning the whole way. Jesse and Frodo stood on the side with their mouths hanging open in shock while Charlie smiled proudly. Just to make sure they wouldn't dare insult her again, Riley tried a bigger jump than she had all day, and she nailed it. She came to a stop right in front of the three guys. Jesse whistled while Charlie and Frodo clapped their hands.

"Sweet run!" Frodo said.

"Yeah, you can keep her," Jesse put in.

"I'll think about it," Charlie said.

"Maybe I'll think about whether to keep *you* around," Riley replied.

Jesse and Frodo cracked up. "I like this girl!" Jesse said, looping an arm around Riley.

Riley was psyched. Who knew it would be so easy to win over a guy who had a face tattoo?

The hours flew by as Riley and Charlie and his friends tore around the skate park. Riley was soon following the guys down some of the really steep drops. The first drop was seriously scary. After that she couldn't get enough. Finally, though, everyone started to get tired, and they all sat down on a bench at the edge of the park to hang.

"Have you guys heard the new Jagged Mask single?" Jesse asked. "They've got a horn section now. Horns! I can't listen to them anymore."

"Why would you bring in horns?" Charlie said. "That makes no sense. What're they trying to do, go mainstream?"

"It's practically R&B now, man," Frodo said sadly. "It's even worse than what happened to Sick Cylinder."

"Hey, I still like Sick Cylinder. They're trying new things, but they're still punk," Charlie said.

"Yeah, maybe," Jesse said. "But why didn't they put that song 'Love Slam' on their last album? It was killer when they played it in concert."

"You know, I heard Damage won't play a gig unless the managers have forty Twinkies backstage before they go on," Frodo said.

"Forty-four, you dweeb," Jesse corrected him. "Eleven for each member of the group."

Wow, Riley thought. They're totally into their bands.

"So, Riley, what do you think of Damage?" Jesse asked.

"I think . . . I think they're fine," she said. It wasn't a lie. She didn't *hate* them, but she barely knew their music. She'd only heard the few songs Charlie had played at the station.

"Riley is not into punk," Charlie explained.

"What *are* you into?" Frodo asked.

"Oh . . . I like Rocketship, All Systems Go—"

Jesse, Frodo, and even Charlie cracked up laughing.

"Dude! You've got a pop princess!" Jesse said, slapping his knee.

"I know. It's tragic," Charlie replied.

Riley shrugged. "I like what I like."

"I bet you listen to Joey Lincoln, too," Frodo said.

Riley couldn't deny it.

"And Barnstormer?" Jesse asked through his laughter.

Okay, can we move on already? Riley thought.

Luckily, Frodo checked his watch. "Uh-oh! It's almost ten. We got late shift at Taco Hut."

"You guys work at Taco Hut?" Riley asked. She actually wasn't all that surprised. Taco Hut was known to be a hangout for skaters and punks. She just couldn't imagine Jesse and Frodo in the brown and orange uniforms and taco-shaped hats.

"Hey, free tacos all the time," Jesse said as he and Frodo grabbed their boards. "Doesn't get better than that."

"Nice to meet you, Riley," Frodo said before they took off on their boards.

"You, too!" Riley called after them. "Your friends are interesting," she said to Charlie as the guys rode out of sight.

"That means you didn't like them?" Charlie asked.

"No! They were great. Especially when they said I was a girly girl and then I shut them up with my rad boarding skills," Riley said.

"Yeah," Charlie agreed. "That *was* pretty cool."

"I should really go, too," Riley said, getting to her feet. "You do not want to see my mom if I'm late for my curfew."

"She goes nuts?" Charlie asked.

"Actually, she kind of looks like that dragon tattoo on Jesse's face," Riley answered.

"I'll walk you home, then," Charlie replied.

They headed up the sand toward the beachfront house Riley, Chloe, their mom, Macy, and their housekeeper, Manuelo, shared. Riley's parents were separated. Her dad now lived in a trailer on the other side of Malibu, mostly doing a lot of yoga, from what Riley and Chloe could tell.

"You know, I still can't believe you like those bands," Charlie said.

"Please! Haven't I been mocked enough already today?" Riley asked.

"Did that bother you? That's just the way those guys are," Charlie said. "Don't take it personally."

"I don't," she assured him. "Besides, I'm already used to *you* dissing my music tastes." A wicked smile lit Riley's face as an idea came to her. "I'll make you a deal," she said. "I will listen to one of your favorite CDs all the way through if you listen to one of mine."

"And then we get to be honest about what we think?" Charlie asked.

"Honesty is key," Riley stated.

"It's a deal," Charlie said.

"So, listen, remember how I told you I'd help you with ideas for Fracture?" Riley went on.

"Yep. You said you had a brilliant creative mind," Charlie reminded her.

Riley grinned. "Well, how about a trivia contest? I thought of it while you and your friends were talking about your favorite bands. You guys could make up the questions and run the competition. And whoever wins could get a gift certificate as a prize."

They had reached Riley's front door. Charlie paused on the step, thinking it over.

"Well? What do you think?" Riley asked excitedly.

"I think it's awesome, and I think my dad will agree," Charlie said.

"Yes!" Riley cheered.

"You *do* have a brilliant creative mind," Charlie told her.

Then he leaned forward to kiss her good-night, and Riley felt as if her feet were floating three inches off the ground. Three kisses in one night *and* she'd solved Charlie's father's business problem. She was on a roll!

# chapter
## five

"**C**hloe! What are you doing?" Quinn demanded.

Chloe was so startled, she almost dropped her nail polish wand on the floor.

"What?" she asked.

"That's Miss Scarlet. You can't put Miss Scarlet on your toenails when you just put Peaches and Cream on your fingernails," Quinn said. "You're going to clash."

Chloe looked down at the streak of red nail polish across her big toe's nail. She hadn't even realized she'd picked up the bottle of Miss Scarlet.

Quinn, Tara, and Amanda were all staring at her through green avocado face masks that matched her own.

Chloe sighed. "I guess I got distracted staring at the clock," she said. She picked up a cotton ball and the bottle of nail polish remover. "Riley's going to miss curfew."

"I could have told you that," Tara said, returning to

filing her nails. "Charlie Slater does not seem like the type who brings his dates home on time."

"I have a bad feeling about this," Chloe said, choosing a cocoa color that coordinated better with the peach. "Does anyone else think Charlie is a little . . ."

"Strange?" Tara supplied for her.

"Well, antisocial or something," Chloe said. "He didn't get up off his butt once all day at the Beach House."

"Maybe he thinks he's too good for Jonah Bayou," Quinn put in.

"Maybe he's just not a good dancer or something," Amanda suggested.

"Okay, but then why come at all?" Chloe said. "He totally brought the place down. And I barely saw Riley all day. She couldn't possibly have had any fun."

At that moment the door to Riley and Chloe's bedroom opened, and Riley walked in. She stared dreamily at the ceiling and almost put her foot into the bowl of avocado mask that was sitting on the floor.

"Riley, stop!" Chloe cried out. She dove over and pulled the bowl out of the way.

Riley laughed. "Thanks, Chloe. I don't think my foot needs a facial."

Chloe glanced at her friends. Riley looked completely dazed.

"So, how was your date?" Chloe asked.

Riley plopped down onto her bed, bouncing up and down.

"It was *so* much fun," she said. "We went skateboarding and had ice cream, and then Charlie's friends Frodo and Jesse showed up."

"Wait a minute. *Frodo*?" Chloe asked.

"Yeah. He was really funny. But you should see Jesse. He has this tattoo of a dragon that goes up his neck and onto his right cheek," Riley said. "It's so cool."

[Chloe: Okay, why does my sister have stars in her eyes right now? She's talking about hanging out with a guy who has a face tattoo and another who's probably got fur between his toes. This is more serious than I thought.]

"You're kidding, right?" Chloe said. "A face tattoo?"

"I know. I was a little freaked at first, but he's nice once you get to know him. And funny," Riley said. "He and Frodo both work at Taco Hut."

"Isn't Taco Hut that place where all the freaks hang out?" Chloe asked.

"Yeah. The one on the boardwalk that everyone walks by a little faster," Amanda said.

"That's the place, but I bet it's not that bad," Riley said. "Jesse and Frodo eat there every day."

"Ew. I hope they didn't breathe on you," Quinn said.

"Oh, please," Riley said, rolling her eyes. "I thought they were cool. And Charlie and I had a very romantic night. He kissed me. Three times."

"Really?" Chloe said. "That's so great."

41

She smiled, happy for her sister, who was clearly falling hard. But inside she just did not get it. Skateboarding and ice cream? Chilling with Frodo and Mr. Face Tattoo? How was that romantic?

**[Chloe: My sister has been brainwashed by skate freaks!]**

"So, are you coming to the Beach House on Monday?" Chloe asked as Riley started to get ready for bed. Normally she would have assumed Riley would be there, but with Charlie in the picture, Chloe wasn't so sure. What if her sister wanted to spend the day chowing down on Mondo Tacos with the skater-boys?

"Wouldn't miss it," Riley said.

"Is Charlie coming?" Quinn asked.

Chloe held her breath.

"No. He has to work at his dad's store," Riley said.

"Oh. That's too bad," Chloe said.

Inside she was actually kind of glad that Charlie wouldn't be joining them again. He clearly didn't have fun, and Riley clearly had less fun with him there. Now at least Chloe would get to hang out with her sister all day, and Riley would get to enjoy the Beach House.

It was the best thing for everybody.

"I got it! I got it!" Chloe called out as the volleyball came sailing toward her. She jumped up and smacked the ball hard with her palm. On the other side of the net

Lennon and another guy both dove for it. Both missed. The volleyball hit the sand, and Chloe's team cheered.

"Nice spike!" Riley said, slapping five with Chloe.

"Nice set!" Chloe returned. She grinned as her team rotated. The sun was shining, the music was pumping, and Chloe and Riley's all-girl team was killing Lennon's all-boy team in the *Teen Scene* Beach House Volleyball Challenge. Could life *be* any better?

"Team Double Trouble wins the serve back!" Jonah Bayou shouted. He was keeping score as cameramen hovered all around the court.

"Isn't this so much more fun than skating with the alt-rock tattoo boys?" Chloe asked Riley.

Riley picked up the ball and grinned, then served an ace over the net. The ball was so smoking, no one could touch it.

"I'll take that as a yes," Chloe said.

"Point to Team Double Trouble!" Jonah called out. "If they make this next point, they advance to the finals!"

"Sweet serve," Seth called to Riley from across the court. "But I bet you can't do it again."

"Just watch me," Riley shouted back.

The ball came bouncing over to her, and she served again. This time one of the guys got a piece of it, but it went bouncing off his hand into the stands. The crowd went wild.

"Team Double Trouble wins!" Jonah Bayou called. "They'll be meeting the D-Boys in the finals!"

Chloe slapped hands with Riley, Quinn, Tara, and their other two teammates.

"Nice game," Lennon said, ducking under the net with Seth.

"Yeah. Who knew you had such a good arm?" Seth said, grinning at Riley.

"You guys played pretty well, too," Riley said, her eyes shining. "Just not good enough!"

"Oh! That hurts. That hurts," Seth said, but he was laughing. "I'd just like to see you try it on the basketball court. That's my game. Not volleyball."

"Excuses, excuses," Riley said, smiling.

"Come on, you guys. Let's get some lemonade before the final match," Chloe suggested.

Riley glanced down at her watch and winced. "I'm sorry, you guys, but you'll have to find a sub for me."

"What? Why?" Chloe asked.

"I didn't realize how late it was," Riley replied. "I told Charlie I'd help him with the signs for the trivia contest tonight."

Chloe looked around at her friends, who were all listening in. "Riley, could I talk to you for a sec?" she asked, tilting her head.

Riley and Chloe walked off toward the sidelines. "I can't believe you're going to leave and miss the final game," Chloe said.

"You guys will have no problem finding a sub," Riley told her.

"It's not that. It's just that I thought you were having fun," Chloe said. "Do you really want to hang out in some dark hole with Moody Boy instead of playing volleyball on the beach?"

The second the words left Chloe's mouth, she realized she'd gone too far. Riley's face fell.

"Do you really think Charlie is moody?" Riley asked.

"No. It's not that. Not really," Chloe said. "It's just . . . you're not into anything he likes, and he's not into anything you like. So what do you see in the guy?"

"He's interesting and smart and funny," Riley said. "And, besides, it gets boring if you agree on everything."

"I guess," Chloe said, not quite sure she understood.

"I know! Why don't you come to the contest tonight at Fracture?" Riley suggested. "I bet if you spend a little time with Charlie, you'll see why I like him."

Chloe looked at her doubtfully.

"Please?"

"Okay, sounds like a plan," Chloe said at last. If Riley was going to be spending so much time with this guy, then Chloe definitely wanted to get to know him better.

"You're the best!" Riley said, hugging her sister. "I'll see you there at seven o'clock!" Then she took off across the beach at a jog.

"Okay! Seven o'clock! Fracture!" Chloe called after her sister, waving.

Now there was just one problem. What should a girl wear to a place called *Fracture*?

# chapter
## six

That night as Chloe and Riley set off for Fracture, Chloe knew she had outdone herself with her outfit. She'd ripped the collar off one of her black T-shirts, giving it a frayed, off-the-shoulder neckline. She wore it over a black tank top and a pair of red plaid Capris with black combat boots. After adding a little hair spray and a ton of black eyeliner, she was ready. At the last minute she chopped the fingertips off a pair of old black gloves and threw them on.

Total punker chic.

"You look great," Riley said as they crossed the street to Fracture. The small store had tons of albums and posters and stickers covering the window. "Thanks for coming with me."

"Hey, what are sisters for?" Chloe replied with a grin.

Riley and Chloe walked into the store. It was bigger

than it looked from the outside. Shelves of CDs, records, and tapes lined the walls and formed rows straight toward the back. A counter along the far wall held sandwiches and munchies. A few tables were set up by a low stage. Chloe was pleasantly surprised. A place that sold barbecue potato chips couldn't be *all* bad.

Charlie stood behind a high counter at the front, ringing up CDs for a pink-haired girl.

"Hey, workaholic!" Riley said.

"Hey!" Charlie replied. His eyes flicked over to them and then quickly flashed back to Chloe.

Chloe felt her face redden. Was something wrong with her outfit?

"Chloe! You look . . . intense," Charlie said. He finished his sale and walked over to them. "Very punk princess."

"Thanks," Chloe said, brightening. "Are you stoked about the contest?"

"Absolutely," Charlie said. He crooked his arm around Riley's neck. "Your sister is a genius. Everyone on the boardwalk has been talking about it all day."

Chloe was impressed that Charlie gave Riley credit for the contest. Maybe he wasn't so bad after all.

"Really?" Riley asked, excited.

"We're expecting a huge turnout," Charlie told her. "So thanks."

"See? Told you I was brilliant," Riley joked.

"Speaking of big turnouts." Charlie looked over his shoulder at the line that was quickly forming at the register. "I'd better get back."

Charlie returned to work, and Chloe and Riley checked out a display of bracelets and necklaces on the counter.

"I knew it! You like him!" Riley said, nudging Chloe. "I can tell by your face."

"He seems cool," Chloe said. "I just want to make sure he's good enough for my little sister," she added. Chloe was born eight minutes before Riley and never let her forget it.

"Gee, thanks," Riley said, rolling her eyes. "Am I ever going to live down those eight minutes?"

"Never," Chloe said. She picked up a black leather bracelet with five turquoise beads at the center. "Oh. This is so you," she said.

Riley reached out and fingered the smooth stones. "I love it!" Then she turned over the price tag and made a face. "Too rich for my wallet."

"Maybe Charlie can get you a discount," Chloe said, noticing Charlie glancing their way.

"Chloe! I'm not going to ask him for that. They're trying to bring customers in, not give stuff away."

"Hey!" someone shouted. "It's the skate chick of the century!"

A scruffy-looking guy came running into the store and practically tackled Riley. He stank of onions. Chloe was about to scream when she realized Riley was laughing.

"Hey, Frodo," Riley said.

He was followed by a guy who seemed more mellow—except for the dragon tattoo all over his face.

"You guys, this is my sister, Chloe," Riley said. "Riley, this is Frodo and Jesse."

Frodo smiled and lifted a hand, but Jesse took one look at Chloe and laughed loudly.

"Nice outfit," he said, looking away.

Chloe glanced down at her clothes. Who did this guy think he was, insulting her like that? Wasn't *he* the one with amateur body art all over his skin?

"Yeah, real punk," Frodo said with a smirk.

"Hey, cut it out!" Riley said. "I think it looks great."

Chloe, for the first time, realized that Riley hadn't so much as changed a hair on her head to come to Fracture. She was wearing a green tank top and her favorite beat-up jeans. Normal Riley gear.

"So, what kind of music do you listen to, Chloe?" Jesse asked with an amused expression. Chloe opened her mouth to answer, but he threw out his hands like stop signs. "No! Don't tell me! I bet you're a huge Nariah fan!"

"As a matter of fact, I—"

"Please! All that girl does is lip-sync and dance. And she does both badly," Jesse said.

Frodo cracked up laughing, and he and Jesse slapped hands.

"You guys, lay off," Charlie said, joining them from behind the counter.

Chloe was relieved that Charlie was taking her side, but she could have sworn she saw him trying not to smile.

"Come on. We're getting ready for the contest," Charlie said.

He, Frodo, and Jesse took the lead, making their

way through the rows of CDs toward the back of the store.

"Just ignore them," Riley whispered to Chloe as they followed.

"How can I? They're horrible," Chloe grumbled. She couldn't believe Charlie was friends with guys like that.

"They'll chill out once they get to know you, I promise," Riley said.

"Great," Chloe said. But she didn't want them to get to know her. She had enough friends. She didn't need approval from a couple of rude punk-music snobs.

Still, she'd promised Riley she would make an effort tonight, and she intended to do just that. It was just one night. How much worse could it get?

Twenty minutes later Chloe felt a surge of relief when Frodo and Jesse went up to the makeshift stage to run the contest. She had managed to ignore them since sitting down at a table, but she was totally tense the whole time, just waiting for the next snarky comment. At least now she could relax and do what she had come here to do—get to know her sister's boyfriend.

Charlie went to the snack bar and grabbed bottles of water for her and Riley. Chloe smiled. At least *he* was turning out to be the good guy Riley promised. They sat back to watch the contest.

It was run like a spelling bee. Each contestant got a question. If he or she answered correctly, he or she stayed in the game. If that person got it wrong, he or she was eliminated and had to go sit in the audience.

"Okay, who was the first bassist for Asylum?" Jesse asked a girl with long black braids and a nose piercing.

"Liam Carson," she said.

"That is correct!" Frodo cheered. "Back in line!"

The girl smiled and stepped back.

The next contestant was old enough to be Chloe's grandfather.

"Where was Scott Grotske born?" Jesse asked him.

"Who's Scott Grotske?" Chloe whispered.

Charlie let out a groan. "The lead singer of Purple Slice," he said. He made a face, like it was *so* obvious.

Riley shrugged at Chloe, and Chloe sat back. She'd never even *heard* of Purple Slice.

Did Charlie really have to act like he was so superior just because he knew about all these punk bands? Why was that so important anyway? He probably wouldn't know who the lead singer of Barnstormer was if she asked him, but she wouldn't be mean to him about it.

"Uh . . . Winnipeg?" the old man answered.

"EEEEEEHHH! Wrong!" Frodo called out obnoxiously. "Get off the stage, mister!"

"How rude," Chloe said, appalled.

"They're just messing around," Charlie told her.

Chloe noticed a couple of punk girls who had been eliminated earlier sitting at the next table. They kept looking her up and down and smirking. She *so* didn't belong here, and she was more than ready to go home.

She glanced at the stage. Only three contestants left.

"Well, it looks like we have a three-way tie!" Jesse said. "What are we going to do about this situation?"

Whatever it is, let's get it over with, Chloe thought. I have some major eyeliner removal to take care of.

"I have an idea!" Frodo called out.

Frodo whispered something in Jesse's ear, and they both grinned. Then Jesse jumped off the stage and made his way toward Chloe, Riley, and Charlie's table.

"Bonus question!" he shouted, stopping behind Chloe.

She looked at her sister, her eyes wide. What was going on?

"Chloe, would you mind standing up?" Frodo asked from the stage.

With everyone staring at her, Chloe did as she was asked. She tried to smile and go with it, but she had no idea what she was going *with*.

"Okay, contestants," Jesse said. He pointed at Chloe. "Is this girl: A) a punk or B) a phony?"

Everyone in the store cracked up. Everyone except Chloe, Riley, and Charlie. Chloe felt her face turning scarlet. They were all laughing at her! She was totally humiliated.

"Riley, can we go now?" Chloe asked through her teeth as Jesse made his way back to the stage.

Riley looked at Chloe, then at Charlie, then back at Chloe again.

Chloe felt something inside her go cold with shock. She could see that her sister felt torn. She couldn't believe it. Was Riley really considering staying here with these jerks? Was she really going to make Chloe walk out alone?

# chapter
## seven

"**L**et's go," Riley said, standing up abruptly. She had waited a split second for Charlie to apologize, or to at least say *something*. When she realized it was actually not going to happen, she knew Chloe was right. It was time to leave.

"Wait. You're going?" Charlie asked.

Jesse and Frodo continued with the trivia contest as if they hadn't just done the meanest thing ever. Everyone in the place was watching the stage again.

"Frodo and Jesse have been rude to Chloe all night," Riley said. "And now they just trashed her in front of everyone else. Why should we stay?"

Riley felt even worse about the whole thing because she had convinced Chloe to come to Fracture. She had told her sister she would have this amazingly great time, and, instead, Chloe was obviously miserable. Riley had unknowingly set Chloe up to be totally embarrassed.

[<u>Riley</u>: **Can I get a worst sister T-shirt please? Size extra-small?**]

"Riley, don't make a big deal out of this," Charlie said, half-standing. "It's just them. They're just teasing."

"Well, they took it too far," Riley said, her arms folded. "That was complete public humiliation. And if you don't see that, then I don't see the point in talking about it anymore."

With that she and Chloe turned and walked out of Fracture. Outside, the cool evening air hit Riley's face, and she felt an ache deep inside. What a disaster! There was no way to undo this. She had just walked out on Charlie. She had no choice, she told herself. Who knew he could be such a jerk?

"I'm so sorry, Chloe," Riley said.

"It's not your fault," Chloe said, slipping an arm around her sister's shoulders. "I'm sorry about Charlie."

"Yeah," Riley said sadly. "Me, too."

Riley sat on the deck of her house, writing in her journal about everything that had just happened. She couldn't make sense of any of it. She had thought that under Charlie's sarcasm there was a nice, sweet, sensitive guy. But apparently under the sarcasm there was just more sarcasm. How could she have been so wrong?

*Chloe's never going to want to hang out with him again, and I don't blame her,* Riley wrote. *And how can I go out with a guy if Chloe doesn't like him? It would be like trying to eat peanut butter in front of her—the smell alone makes her go green. It's just not done.*

Riley sighed and looked out at the crashing ocean. She wasn't even sure *she* was going to want to hang out with Charlie and his friends again. She couldn't be comfortable around Jesse and Frodo after what they had done to her sister.

But whenever she thought about Charlie—especially when she thought about their second kiss—her heart hurt. That moment had been so completely perfect. And she loved spending time with him when they were alone together. He made her laugh, and he made her think. Was she really never going to be with him again?

"Hey."

Riley jumped at the sound of Charlie's voice. He was standing at the outside stairs to the deck, looking forlorn.

[<u>Riley</u>: **Don't just give in, right? We all know he was a total jerk, and I should probably never talk to him again. Ever. Oh . . . but why is my heart suddenly pounding so hard? And why does he have to be so cute?**]

She crossed her arms over her chest and raised her eyebrows at him. "What are you doing here?"

"I came to say I'm sorry," Charlie said, climbing the steps toward her. "I'm really, really sorry for what happened tonight."

"As long as you're really, *really* sorry," Riley said sarcastically.

"Okay, I guess I deserve that," Charlie said. "Look, I should have told the guys off the second they did that to your sister. And I want you to know that I did tell them they were idiots. I told them right after you left."

Riley looked up at him. "Really?"

"Yeah. I can't believe how mean they were," Charlie said. "But I was no better. I feel like such a jerk."

Riley's heart warmed as Charlie's big brown eyes pleaded with her. She couldn't help it. This was the sensitive-underneath guy she knew and liked!

"Well, I'm not really the one who needs to be apologized to," she said, not wanting to give in just yet.

"I'll apologize to Chloe, too, I swear," Charlie said. "I want to. That's half of why I came over here."

"And the other half?" Riley asked.

Charlie blew out a long breath, and when he spoke, his voice was hoarse. "Don't you know?" he asked. "You."

Riley cracked a small smile. "All right then. I guess I'll keep you around."

Charlie's whole face lit up. "Yeah?"

"Yeah," Riley said.

"Good." Charlie sat down on the end of her chaise lounge. "Then I can give you this." He pulled something out of his jacket pocket and held it out to her.

Riley gasped. It was the turquoise bracelet she and Chloe had admired at the store earlier that night.

"I love it!" she said.

"I know. I overheard you talking about it," he said.

"Are you sure it's okay?" Riley asked. "I mean, if the store isn't doing so well—"

"Thanks to you, tonight was our biggest sales night in a year," Charlie said with a laugh. "Consider the bracelet a thank-you."

Riley grinned. "Well, when you put it that way . . ."

She held out her arm, and Charlie fastened the bracelet around her wrist. Riley held it up. The blue stones glistened in the moonlight.

"Thanks, Charlie," she said.

Charlie smiled and held her hand. "Thanks for being so cool about everything."

Riley shrugged, her heart beating rapidly. "No problem," she said.

[<u>Riley</u>: **What I didn't say was that working things out with Charlie felt so right. The other thing I didn't say? That this time I really wanted that feeling to last.**]

Chloe took two bowls from a kitchen cabinet and dropped a couple of spoons into them. Then she gathered them up in her arms along with the carton of frozen yogurt, the strawberries, chocolate sauce, whipped cream, sprinkles, and chocolate chips. This was definitely a night for a chowdown. She was just thanking her lucky stars that Manuelo had recently gone shopping.

She turned, carefully balancing everything as she headed for the living room. Riley would be in from her nightly journal venting any minute, and then they were going to spend the next two hours watching a vintage Madonna movie and stuffing themselves.

On the way into the living room, Chloe heard voices and paused. She looked out onto the deck and stared in disbelief. Charlie was out there. And he and Riley were kissing!

Chloe almost dropped the frozen yogurt and toppings. How could Riley have forgiven him so quickly? After everything that happened, Chloe thought her sister had finally woken up and smelled the incompatibility. But from the looks of things, the girl had fallen right back into her punk-rocker daze.

Dropping everything onto the coffee table in the living room, Chloe turned to go outside. She needed to talk to Riley about this. Charlie was no good for her. There were about a million other guys out there who were ten times more Riley's type. But she stopped halfway across the room. Riley and Charlie were now holding hands and giggling. Was she really going to walk out there and say, "Lay off my sister, sleaze-boy"?

That would work out well, Chloe thought. Not. She was just going to have to wait for Charlie to leave. Then she and Riley could have a heart-to-heart.

She sat down on the couch, flicked on the TV, and started to make herself a sundae. Charlie couldn't stay out there forever. Could he?

# chapter
# eight

"**I** can't believe they did that to you!" Tara cried.

Chloe, Tara, Amanda, and Quinn were gathered in a corner of the Beach House's huge party room. Chloe had just told her friends about the scene at Fracture the night before.

"If I ever meet those guys, they are in for the hissy fit of the century," Tara promised.

"And Riley forgave Charlie? She must be brainwashed or something," Quinn put in.

"You definitely have to wonder," Chloe said. At least her friends agreed with her. She watched as some girl got way low under the limbo stick on the dance floor. Jonah was running a limbo contest, and it was down to two people, one of whom was Larry Slotnick.

"Well, Charlie did apologize to me before he left," Chloe added, trying to be fair.

"So? He should've gotten up and booted his freaky

friends out of the store right then and there!" Tara cried.

"Yeah!" Quinn agreed.

"Where is Riley, anyway?" Amanda asked.

"She's spending the day with Charlie," Chloe said with a sigh.

"Doing what?" Quinn asked.

"Getting a tongue piercing?" Chloe suggested.

"She wouldn't!" Tara said.

"No, of course she wouldn't," Chloe said. "I was just kidding."

As Larry made another go at the limbo stick, Chloe wondered what Riley and Charlie were doing just then. Were they skateboarding? Hanging out at Fracture? What else did guys like Charlie do for fun? Whatever it was, she had a feeling it was something Riley had never done before. It was probably something Riley had never even *thought* about doing before.

"They have nothing in common," Chloe said, honestly confused. "What could they possibly be doing together?"

"Search me," Quinn said.

The whole crowd reacted with an "Oh!" as the last of the girls in the limbo contest fell. Then Larry went again and practically twisted himself into a pretzel to get under the stick. It looked as if his chin was going to hit the bar, but at the last second he tipped his head back and made it under. The Beach House went wild. Chloe and her friends were impressed. They all clapped like mad.

"I declare Larry Slotnick the King of Limbo!" Jonah Bayou announced. He grabbed Larry's wrist and thrust his arm in the air.

Larry jumped up and down, cheering. Seconds later he was surrounded by beautiful girls who hugged and kissed him as the cameras recorded it all. Larry blushed bright red but couldn't stop grinning.

Chloe laughed. Riley would have *loved* to see this.

"Who knew Larry could be king of anything?" Tara asked.

"He did great," Amanda said.

With the contest over, Chloe and her friends headed for the snack bar to get drinks. Chloe sat down on one of the wooden bar stools, her mind already back on The Problem.

Quinn knew what she was thinking about. "So, what are you going to do about Riley?" Quinn asked as Tara ordered up some smoothies.

"I don't know," Chloe said, looking out across the dance floor. "I just don't get it. I mean, right now I see at least ten guys who are so much more her type. I bet Riley would have more fun with any one of them than with Charlie."

"Yeah. Too bad she's not even here to meet them," Amanda agreed.

Tara handed each of them a smoothie, and they all settled in to people-watch.

Chloe took one sip of her cold orange-raspberry

concoction, and then it hit her—the greatest idea she'd ever had.

"That's it! I've got it!" she announced.

"Wow. That's one powerful smoothie," Tara said, eyes wide.

"Tell me about it," Chloe said, turning in her seat to face her friends. "I am going to find Riley her ultimate man. He's got to be in this Beach House somewhere. And once Riley meets him, she'll realize what I've known all along."

"That Charlie is totally wrong for her?" Quinn suggested.

"Exactly," Chloe said with a grin.

"I don't know, Chloe," Amanda said thoughtfully. "I mean, I get that you don't like him, but it seems like Riley really does."

"Yeah. Do you really think she's going to dump him just because a different guy comes along?" Tara asked.

"Not just different, more *Riley*," Chloe said. "I'm talking about Mr. Perfect-for-Riley-Carlson."

"And what about Charlie?" Quinn said. "I know the guy's freaky and all, but he's going to be crushed."

"Please. He'll bounce back and ask out some punk chick, and then even he'll be better off," Chloe said, refusing to be brought down. "This is really the best plan for everyone."

"It could work," Tara said thoughtfully.

"It will. All we have to do is find the perfect guy,"

Chloe said. She had never felt so sure of anything.

At that moment Larry samba-ed over to them with a huge sombrero on his head. Multicolored ribbons decorated the straw cone, and dozens of felt disks hung from the brim.

"What is that thing?" Chloe asked.

"This, my girl, is the crown of the Limbo King!" Larry announced, doing a little spin that almost knocked him off his feet. He steadied himself and the hat, the felt disks dancing back and forth. "So, what are you *chicas* talking about?"

"We're on a mission," Chloe told him, looking past his shoulder at a blond surfer type on the dance floor. "We are going to find Riley the perfect guy."

"Ooo! Ooo! I'll do it! I'm in!" Larry said, raising a hand and bouncing up and down in front of them. The disks on his hat bobbed like rubber balls.

Chloe laughed and rolled her eyes. "Thanks, Larry, but I don't think so. This guy has to be . . . perfect."

Larry's face fell, and he sat down next to Chloe. "But I'm the King of Limbo," he said, sulking.

"I know," Chloe said, patting him on the back. "But Riley isn't exactly a limbo queen. Maybe you can help us find the guy."

Larry's face lit up. "That's perfect! Because nobody knows what Riley likes more than I do. I've been following her around since—"

"Second grade. I know. I was there," Chloe reminded

him. She pulled her friends into a huddle, her eyes glinting with mischief. "Okay, you guys, here's the plan. . . ."

"Let's get started," Chloe said. She and her friends were sitting on the canvas-covered couches in the living room of the Beach House. Quinn, Amanda, and Tara sat to her left, Larry to her right. Chloe felt very official. This was, after all, serious business.

Chloe gazed out through the windows of the living room's French doors. She could see most of the other Beach House kids hanging by the pool, the volleyball court, or at the tables on the lawn. "Larry, would you bring in the first contestant?" she asked.

"Check," Larry said. "First contestant, coming right up."

Letting himself out through the French doors, Larry went over to the pool and headed straight for a guy who had just tossed a long Styrofoam noodle to a girl in the water. Chloe remembered him from lunch the other day. He seemed pretty nice. Larry talked to the guy for a moment, and then the guy came inside with him.

The guy had dark hair, brown eyes, and an eager look on his face. He took a seat in an easy chair and looked curiously at what Chloe was starting to think of as The Committee. The Committee to Find Mr. Right for Riley, that is.

"Yo, dude!" Larry said in a voice of authority.

"Yo, yourself," the guy said, smiling.

Chloe, Quinn, and Tara exchanged appreciative looks. He was really quite cute.

"You're David, right?" Chloe asked.

"David Darren," he said.

"So, David, why do you want to date Riley Carlson?" Tara asked, crossing her legs and folding her hands in front of her.

Chloe almost cracked up laughing. Tara looked like the host of a TV talk show. It was the perfect interviewer's pose.

"Well, that guy," David said, pointing at Larry, "told me Riley was the most beautiful woman in the world. Who wouldn't want a chance to date the most beautiful woman in the world?"

"Uh—he might have been exaggerating a *little*," Chloe admitted, hoping Larry hadn't overdone it. "But Riley is totally great," she added quickly.

David flashed a grin, and Chloe smiled, impressed. Could they have found the right guy on the very first try?

Then David reached into his pocket and pulled out something green. Something green and slimy-looking. Something green and slimy-looking that was *moving*.

"What do you think, Rico?" David asked, bringing the slimy thing up near his face and talking to it. "Don't you think we deserve a shot at the most beautiful woman in the world?"

"What *is* that thing?" Chloe asked, shrinking back into the sofa cushions.

"This is my lizard, Rico," David explained. He placed the lizard on his shoulder, where it started to crawl around. It went up his neck and sat down on top of his head. Then it looked at Chloe and stuck out its long tongue. "I take Rico everywhere I go," David said.

"NEXT!" Chloe, Tara, Amanda, and Quinn cried in unison.

David was followed by a blond guy who had just done a gorgeous jackknife off the high board. He had broad shoulders and a loping walk. He looked kind of blank and dazed to Chloe, but she went ahead with the questions.

"You are . . . ?" she asked.

"Beach Wilson," he said.

"Age?" Quinn piped up.

"Sixteen," he said.

"Beach, why don't you tell us about your idea of the perfect date?" Chloe said.

"Oh . . . wow," Beach said with a goofy laugh. "That's a tough one. Um . . . I'd have to say . . . March eleventh. That's my birthday, and my mom always makes this killer cake with this frosting she does from scratch."

Chloe looked at her girlfriends. Was he *kidding*?

"NEXT!" they shouted.

"Wait! I wanted to hear more about the cake!" Larry said as Beach loped off.

"Larry, we're here for Riley, remember?" Chloe said. "Let's bring in the next guy."

Larry went back outside. Chloe brightened when he returned with the next candidate. The guy walking into the living room was tall with strong-looking arms, a bright smile, and the bluest blue eyes she'd ever seen. His blond hair was long in front and short in back, and he was carrying a surfboard under one arm. This could be the guy they were looking for.

"Name?" Chloe asked.

"Austin Hatcher," he said.

"Age?" Tara asked.

"Sixteen."

"I see you're a surfer, Austin," Chloe said, leaning forward.

"Oh, yeah. It's been such a beautiful week. I've been out there every morning before coming here," he said.

"Austin, why do you want to date Riley Carlson?" Quinn asked.

Austin blushed in an adorable way. "Well, actually, I go to West Malibu, and I've seen Riley around. I think she's cool, and I've always wanted to ask her out. I've just never gotten up the guts."

Chloe's heart stirred. How sweet was this guy? Larry shifted on the couch, and Chloe saw that he was scowling for some reason, but she chose to ignore it.

"Do you have any hobbies besides surfing?" Amanda asked.

"I play soccer in the fall. And I also paint," Austin replied. "Everyone needs a creative outlet, right?"

Goose bumps popped up all over Chloe's arms. This guy was *made* for Riley. She could feel it. But there was still one more question.

"Austin, what's your idea of a perfect date?" she asked.

"Well, it all really depends on the girl, because you want to do something she would enjoy doing," he said.

Chloe smiled. She knew Riley would love that answer.

"But if it were totally up to me," Austin went on, "I guess I'd pack a romantic picnic and go to the beach to watch the sun set."

At this point Larry's foot was bouncing up and down like crazy.

"And then I'd take her hand, and we'd go for a walk along the water . . ."

Larry cleared his throat a few times, and Chloe noticed his face was turning purple.

"And then, if she seemed like she wanted me to, I'd give her a good-night kiss under the stars—"

"That's it! I can't listen to this anymore!" Larry exploded, standing up. Before Chloe could grab him, he got right in Austin's face.

"Yeah, yeah, romance is all well and good, but are you going to carry her surfboard and books for her every day?" Larry demanded. "Will you call her every single night?"

Austin leaned back a bit, obviously scared.

"Larry!" Chloe hissed.

Larry ignored her. "Will you save every last one of her empty yogurt containers and keep them on a shrine shelf next to your bed?" he asked, his eyes wide. "Well? Will you?"

"Um, I think I'd better go," Austin said.

Then he rushed back out of the Beach House faster than Chloe could say "See ya!"

"Yeah! I didn't think so!" Larry called after him, looking proud of himself.

"Larry!" Tara and Quinn screeched.

"How could you do that?" Amanda asked.

"What? He was so not worthy of my Riley!" Larry said.

Chloe's head hit the back of the couch. This was not exactly going the way she'd planned.

# chapter
## nine

"Are you sure it's safe around here?" Riley asked Charlie as they rounded a corner in Lakaya Beach. Everyone knew Lakaya Beach was a bad neighborhood. And here was Charlie, walking her right into it.

He laughed and took her hand, sending goose bumps up her arm. "I hang out here all the time," he said. "It's cool."

Riley relaxed a bit after seeing how laid-back Charlie was. If he could hang out here, she could hang out here. She just wished it didn't seem as if people were staring at them all the way down the street. Hadn't they ever seen two people holding hands before?

"Where are we going, again?" Riley asked.

"This girl, Lily, is having a party," Charlie said. "The landlord of her building lets her use the basement. Wait till you see it. It's totally crazy."

"No doubt," Riley said, wondering what kind of

party Charlie considered "totally crazy." Well, she was about to find out. A date with Charlie was definitely an adventure.

She decided to ignore the little nervous twinge she felt in the pit of her stomach. "So," she said, "I came up with another idea for Fracture, if you're interested."

"Sure," Charlie said. "What've you got for me this time, O Brilliant One?"

"I was thinking you guys could have an Open Mike night. You know, where anyone can go onstage and perform music or tell jokes or whatever," Riley explained. "There are a lot of out-of-town people in West Malibu right now because of the *Teen Scene* thing. I figure an Open Mike night could bring in a ton of people who've never even *heard* of Fracture."

Charlie smiled, impressed. "I like it," he said. "I'll check with my dad when I get home."

"Cool," Riley said.

"How did I ever luck out with you?" Charlie said.

Then, much to Riley's surprise, he picked her up off her feet and twirled her around. A couple of guys on the street hooted and whistled. Riley blushed and laughed as she hit the ground again. Charlie was always surprising her. It was one of the things she liked best about him.

"We're here," Charlie said a few minutes later. He stopped in front of a broken-down stucco building.

There was a boarded-up window on the bottom floor, and the outside stairs were all cracked. Riley could hear music blaring from the basement.

"We're where?" she asked, looking around nervously. "The local jail?"

"Ha-ha," Charlie said. Then he grabbed her hand and dragged her down the stairs.

The inside of the basement was like nothing Riley had ever seen. It took her eyes a moment to adjust to the darkness. When they did, she saw that there were about forty people in the room, dancing, shouting, and laughing. Graffiti covered the concrete walls, and a couple of guys stood near the door, adding to the artwork with cans of spray paint. The music was deafening and seemed to be coming from huge speakers on all sides. As Riley and Charlie looked around, a group of kids ran screaming past them, chasing each other, then tackling themselves into a pile in the corner.

[**Riley**: Okay, this is not a party. It's a WWE SmackDown! What am I doing here?]

"Want to dance?" Charlie asked.

Before Riley could manage a response, he'd pulled her to the center of the dance floor. Riley's jaw dropped as Charlie started to move to the beat of the music. Charlie could dance! He was actually pretty good.

Once she got past being stunned, Riley let herself get into the dancing. Soon she forgot where she was and started to totally enjoy herself. Dancing with Charlie was the best. He even twirled and dipped her, making Riley crack up laughing. The twirls didn't exactly go with the screeching guitar and angry lyrics, but that just made them even funnier.

"Nice moves!" a familiar voice shouted.

Riley cringed as Jesse and Frodo pushed toward them. Seeing them made her remember the awful way they'd treated Chloe last night. That brought her right back down to Earth.

"Hey, Riley! Where's your sister? She'd fit right in here!" Jesse said sarcastically. He and Frodo laughed and slapped hands.

"You think you're so funny," Riley said. "Well, I'm not laughing. And neither was Chloe."

Frodo's face fell. "Sorry," he said. "We were just having a little fun."

"Well, it wasn't fun for her," Riley told them.

"Come on. We didn't mean anything," Jesse added.

"Listen, what if we just forget last night and start over?" Charlie suggested. "I'll go get us some drinks. Why don't you guys find someplace to sit?" He headed off through the crowd.

Riley shrugged and went along with Jesse and Frodo. A bunch of old couches and chairs lined the back wall. One of the couches was empty. They sat down together, and immediately Riley got an uncomfortable feeling in her stomach. No one said a word.

Riley couldn't take this. How was she supposed to date Charlie if just being around his friends made her feel so awful?

"So, what did you guys do today?" Riley asked finally, trying to be nice.

"Worked, mostly," Jesse replied.

"This one guy ordered ten Taco Supremos and ate them *all*," Frodo said, his eyes wide. "I*'ve* never even done that."

"Yeah. It was pretty gross," Jesse said.

"Great," Riley replied.

"Hey, there's Jimmy, the roadie for Starkers!" Frodo said, pointing at a guy with purple spiky hair. "I wanna find out where they're playing next."

"We'll be right back," Jesse told Riley before they both jumped up and headed across the room.

Riley had thought she would never want to be left alone at this party, but she was relieved when they were gone. At least she didn't have to struggle to make conversation anymore.

Riley glanced across the room to see what was keeping Charlie, but she couldn't find him. Instead, her eyes were drawn to a girl about her age who was staring right at her. Riley looked away, then back again. The girl was still staring at her. She was tall with short black hair and a nose piercing. She didn't seem too happy to see Riley sitting there.

After about a minute-long staring match, the girl

walked over and plopped down beside Riley on the couch.

"Hey," she said.

"Hi," Riley replied.

"I'm Lily," she said.

"Oh! This is your party, right?" Riley said. "It's really great."

"Thanks," Lily said. She looked Riley up and down. "Charlie didn't tell you about me, huh?"

Riley blinked. "He told me this was your place."

"He didn't tell you we used to go out?" Lily asked.

"No," Riley said, surprised. Charlie had brought her to his ex-girlfriend's house for a party? That was a little weird.

"Yeah, well, I just thought I'd let you know that you're the rebound girl," Lily said.

"The rebound girl?" Riley repeated.

"Yeah. And the second Charlie realizes you're not his type he's going to dump you," Lily said. "You may as well just save yourself the trouble and go home right now."

Riley sat up a little straighter. Who did this girl think she was? "Really? If I'm so not his type, then why am I here with him and you're not?"

Lily raised her eyebrows, clearly surprised that Riley was standing up for herself.

"Fine. Have fun," Lily said flatly. Then she got up and walked away.

Riley crossed her arms over herself and willed the

uncomfortable feeling in her gut to go away. But it just wouldn't. She felt even worse than she had before. Sure, she had stood up to Lily, but that didn't change the fact that she clearly didn't belong here. Everyone else in the room was talking and dancing and laughing. They were totally in the right place. Riley totally was not.

Could she really make it work with Charlie if she didn't like doing the things he liked to do? If she didn't like his friends? And Charlie didn't enjoy Riley's version of fun either. He was clearly bored at the *Teen Scene* Beach House.

On top of everything, Chloe didn't like hanging out with Charlie. How was Riley going to handle the fact that her sister, who was also her best friend, didn't want to be around her boyfriend?

By the time Charlie returned with her soda, Riley felt sick. She was completely confused. Ten minutes ago she was totally into Charlie, having a great time. It was as if they were the only people in the world. But now it was totally clear that they weren't the only people in the world. There were lots of other people to think of, and none of them seemed to think Charlie and Riley belonged together.

"Wow, you look miserable," Charlie said, standing over her. He sighed and looked at the floor. "I never should have brought you here."

Riley felt a pang in her heart. Even Charlie didn't think she belonged in his life!

"Yeah. Maybe you shouldn't have," Riley said, standing up.

"Riley, hang on a sec—"

"No. It's fine. I clearly don't fit in with your friends, and you clearly don't fit in with mine," Riley said as calmly as possible.

"Riley, why are you freaking out?" Charlie said. "Did something happen?"

"No. And I'm not freaking out. I'm fine," Riley said. "I just don't think this is going to work."

Before she could change her mind or look into Charlie's confused eyes again, Riley turned on her heel and walked out. Jesse, Frodo, and Lily watched her go. She was sure they were all glad she was leaving, but she tried not to think about that. She had made the right decision.

But if that was true, why was she blinking back tears?

# chapter
## ten

Chloe, Tara, Quinn, Amanda, and Larry all slumped back on the couches, exhausted. They had interviewed almost every available guy in the Beach House, and now the sun was starting to go down.

"Did you guys have any luck with your date search?" Jonah Bayou asked, strolling into the living room.

Chloe looked up at him. She was so used to seeing him now, he was like just another guy.

"Hardly," she said. "You wouldn't happen to want the job, would you?"

"Thanks. I would, but I think Nariah would get kind of jealous," Jonah said with a grin. "Good luck, though."

"Thanks," Quinn groaned.

Jonah walked off, and Chloe looked at her friends. "This has been one of longest days of my life," she confessed.

"I can't believe we couldn't find one single guy for Riley," Quinn said with a groan.

"I know!" Amanda said.

"We did find him! It was Austin!" Tara insisted. "We had him right here—until Larry scared him off," she added, narrowing her eyes at Larry.

"Hey! You guys are gonna thank me later. That guy had *serial killer* written all over him," Larry replied.

"Yeah, maybe in La-La Larry Land," Tara shot back.

"You guys! Arguing will get us nowhere," Chloe said. "It won't bring Austin back."

"I don't think a million dollars could bring Austin back," Quinn said.

"We might as well admit it," Chloe said. "We failed. I just don't get it, though. How hard can it be to find a creative, athletic guy who loves the beach and is into good music? I mean, we're in the *Teen Scene* Beach House! You'd think they'd be all over the place."

"Hey, guys! What's up?" Lennon said as he and Seth let themselves in through the French doors. They were wearing T-shirts and sweats, and Lennon had a basketball tucked under his arm.

"Oh . . . nothing," Chloe said with a weak smile. She sat up straight and felt all the muscles in her back twinge. "What's up with you guys? Where have you been all day?"

"We were just playing pickup basketball at the park, and my brother stopped by with today's paper. Check it out," Seth said. "It's so cool."

He showed them a folded newspaper that was open to the "Local Voices" section. Printed at the top of the page was a poem titled "Morning on the Beach" by Seth Rovino.

"You wrote this?" Amanda asked.

"Yep," Seth said proudly. "I sent it in a couple of weeks ago, but I never really thought they'd print it. Even the literary magazine at school rejected it, and I'm on the editorial staff."

Chloe read the poem quickly. "I don't know why they didn't take it," she said. "It's really good."

"Thanks," Seth said.

"We're gonna hit the beach for a quick surf and then head over to the Newsstand," Lennon told them. "There's a soloist tonight that Seth wants to see."

"Really? Who?" Chloe asked.

"His name is Bryan Childs," Seth said. "Plays incredible guitar. He just released an independent album."

"I know! Riley bought one of the first copies," Chloe said.

"You guys want to come?" Lennon asked.

"I need to go home and shower, but I'll meet you guys there later," Chloe offered.

"Great. See you then," Seth said.

Lennon gave Chloe a quick kiss on the cheek and headed out with his friend. The second they were gone, Chloe looked at Quinn, Tara, and Amanda and knew they were thinking the same thing she was.

"Ohmigosh. He's been under our noses the entire time," Chloe said.

"They were totally flirting on the volleyball court the other day," Quinn said.

"And remember the first time we told the guys about the Beach House? It was Riley who told Seth to come," Tara said.

"Maybe she already likes him and she just doesn't realize it," Amanda added.

"It's perfect!" Chloe said, her heart pounding with excitement.

Chloe and her girlfriends stood up and squealed in happiness, hugging each other over a job well done. Seth Rovino. It was so obvious! Any idiot could see he and Riley would be perfect together.

"Um, you guys?" Larry asked, watching them with confusion. "What just happened?"

"Chloe, do you really think it's a good idea to set up Seth and Riley on a date and not even tell Riley about it?" Lennon asked.

They had just left the Newsstand after Bryan Childs's set, and Lennon was walking Chloe home. Chloe had asked Seth about the date at the Newsstand. Seth had seemed excited about the idea. They already had a time arranged.

"Trust me. I know what I'm doing," Chloe told Lennon. "If I told Riley that it was a date, she might not come. But she's going to love me for this later."

"Okay. You know your sister better than I do," Lennon said as they stopped in front of Chloe's door. He still looked doubtful.

"Don't worry. It's going to be great," Chloe reassured him.

Lennon gave her a quick kiss and said good night.

Chloe let herself in and headed upstairs to her room. Riley should have come tonight, Chloe thought. Her sister never would have missed Bryan Childs if it weren't for Charlie. But when she got upstairs, she found Riley lying on her bed, staring at the ceiling. Not a good sign. Something was definitely wrong.

"Hey! What's up?" Chloe asked.

"Charlie and I broke up," Riley said, her voice flat.

"What happened?" Chloe asked, crossing the room quickly.

Riley pushed herself up and shrugged. "I don't know. I just had a feeling it wasn't going to work."

Chloe hugged her sister. "I'm really sorry, Riley," she said. "I mean it. Even if there was something about Charlie I didn't exactly like."

Riley let out a small laugh. "I know. Maybe you were right all along."

Chloe leaned back and looked at her sister's sad face. She felt as if it was her own heart that was broken. But, luckily, Chloe had just the thing to cheer Riley up. The timing couldn't have been more perfect.

"Are you going to come to the Beach House tomorrow?" Chloe asked.

Riley let out a slow sigh. "I don't know. I might not be in the mood. I think I'll be busy staring at the ceiling all day." She flopped back on her pillow again. "Did you know that if you stare at the spot right above my bed long enough, those swirls start to look like Ozzy Osbourne?"

Chloe squinted and looked up. "Wow. You need to move your bed."

"Tell me about it," Riley said.

"About tomorrow—"

"I think I'm just going to go surfing and get some quality alone time," Riley said.

Chloe started to panic. Riley *had* to come to the Beach House. Her whole plan depended on it.

"Alone time is not what you need right now," Chloe said, getting to her feet. "What you need is some serious distraction."

"I don't know, Chloe," Riley said.

"It's totally true! You need something to take your mind off this breakup or you'll go crazy," Chloe told her sister. "It's in all the magazines. It's, like, a clinical condition: Breakup Mopey-itis."

"You made that up," Riley said, but she smiled.

"You have to come. They're having a lip-sync contest," Chloe said. "Larry's going to do 'Baby Got Back.' You *cannot* miss that."

"You have a point there," Riley said, sitting up a bit. "What better way to cure Breakup Mopey-itis than with some good lip-sync therapy?"

"There you go!" Chloe said.

"Okay. I'm in," Riley told her.

"Good," Chloe said. "I promise you won't regret it."

[Chloe: The Set-Riley-Up plan just became the Cheer-Riley-Up plan. Luckily, the timing couldn't be better. Plus we've got the perfect guy for her. It's going to work. How can it not?]

# chapter
## eleven

"**C**ongratulations, Larry," Riley said. "That was the most unique lip-sync routine I've ever seen."

Larry sat down at the table, a silver crown tilting at an angle on his spiky hair. He was wearing black sunglasses, black pants, and a black jacket, and he was sweating buckets after his rap and dance.

"Jonah says if I win one more contest, I take home the triple crown," Larry said. "No one's ever taken home the triple crown before."

"What other contests are left?" Seth asked.

"Somebody said something about a best bod competition," Larry said, whipping off his jacket and flexing his nonexistent biceps.

Everyone at the table laughed. "Oh, yeah. That's a lock," Chloe said.

Riley grinned, but it wasn't easy. Larry was funny, as always, but she wasn't exactly in the mood to laugh. She was trying, but it was hard to be happy after everything that had happened the night before.

Still, it was a beautiful day. And she, Chloe, Amanda, Quinn, Tara, Lennon, Seth, and Larry had snagged one of the best tables in the Beach House's huge, gorgeous party room. It was close to the snack bar but still had a good view of the dance floor. Riley watched a group of kids break dancing a few feet away and tried not to think about Charlie.

"So, Riley, I'm glad you came today," Seth said out of nowhere.

Riley smiled at him. "Thanks. Me, too."

"Well, I don't know about you guys, but that last bottle of water *really* got to me," Chloe said suddenly. "I'm going to the ladies' room. Anyone want to come?"

"Oh . . . yeah! Definitely," Amanda said, standing up with Chloe.

"I really need to . . . check my lip liner," Quinn said, getting up as well.

"I'll come, too," Riley suggested.

"No!" Chloe, Quinn, and Tara all shouted.

Riley was so startled, she sat right back down.

"I'm going to go, and there are only three stalls, so there's really no point in your going until I get back," Tara said quickly.

"Ooookay," Riley said. Sometimes her sister's friends could be really weird.

The foursome headed off toward the bathroom

together. Chloe looked over her shoulder at the table about ten times.

Riley looked around at Seth, Lennon, and Larry. No one said a word. Why was everyone acting so weird?

"Hey, Larry!" Lennon said loudly. "Why don't we go get some sodas?"

"No, thanks," Larry said with a shrug. "I'm good."

Lennon stood up and hovered over Larry. "Yeah, but I *really need* a soda," Lennon said.

"So go ahead and get one," Larry said. He glanced back and forth between Riley and Seth. "I'll just stay here."

Lennon sighed. "Sorry about this, man." He grabbed both of Larry's upper arms and hauled him out of his chair.

Riley ducked as Larry's feet almost hit her head. She and Seth cracked up as Lennon carried Larry all the way over to the snack bar.

"Suddenly I'm *very* thirsty!" Larry called out.

"Okay, what was *that* all about?" Riley asked.

"Who knows?" Seth replied.

"So . . . Chloe told me about your poem being in the paper," Riley said. "That's so great."

"Thanks. It was a total surprise," Seth said.

He seemed a little uncomfortable. Maybe he was just shy when it came to talking about his poetry, Riley thought. Though he hadn't been shy about it the first time she met him.

"Listen, do you want anything?" Seth blurted out. "Something to drink or eat? Because I could get you anything you want."

"No, thanks. I'm fine," Riley said.

"Oh . . . okay." Seth fiddled with his napkin but kept his eyes on Riley.

Something about the way Seth was looking at her made Riley feel tense. It was like he was expecting something. Like he was both a little too excited and a little too nervous.

Riley's stomach started to feel funny again.

"Something wrong?" Seth asked.

Suddenly Riley realized that his hair had more gel in it than was strictly necessary. Plus he was wearing pressed khaki shorts and a button-down shirt. He was just a little too dressed up for a guy on a regular old day at the Beach House.

[**Riley: Wait a minute. First everyone gets up from the table in totally suspicious ways. Then Seth asks if he can get me anything. And now he's looking at me like . . . like any second now a little cartoon Cupid is going to appear over his shoulder and zing an arrow into me. Am I on a date here?**]

"Um . . . no. I'm fine," Riley said.

She glanced toward the bathrooms and saw that Chloe, Amanda, Quinn, and Tara were all huddled by the wall, watching her. The second Riley looked up, they started talking animatedly, as if they hadn't been staring at her.

Oh God. This *is* a date! Riley thought, her face burning. Chloe set me up on a date and didn't even tell me!

"Seth, could you excuse me for a second?" Riley asked.

"Sure," Seth said, his face falling slightly.

Riley walked over to her sister and grabbed her arm. "Would you mind coming with me to the bathroom? It looks like all the stalls are free now," she said.

Chloe gave her friends a panicked look but allowed Riley to drag her into the bathroom.

"Okay. What's going on?" Riley demanded. "Are Seth and I on a date or something?"

"Well . . . kind of," Chloe said.

"Chloe! How could you do this?" Riley exploded.

"Well, excuse me for setting you up with an amazing guy!" Chloe shot back.

"That is so not the point! You didn't even warn me!" Riley said. "And, besides, when did you set this up?"

"Last night at the Newsstand," Chloe said, biting her lip.

"But as far as you knew, I was still with Charlie then!" Riley said.

"Yeah, but you're not with Charlie now. So what's the big deal?" Chloe asked.

Riley sighed. She didn't really have an answer for

that one. She and Charlie were over. She could go out with anyone she wanted. So why did she feel so guilty and awful?

"Look, I know you like Charlie, but you guys weren't getting along," Chloe said. "Can't you just give Seth a chance? I really think you guys will hit it off."

"Maybe you're right," Riley said. "I mean, if I dated Seth, everything would go back to normal. We could hang out here and at the beach and at the Newsstand. . . ."

"No more weird underground parties or evil ex-girlfriends," Chloe put in. "No more freaky, dragon-faced skater boys."

"Nothing unexpected," Riley said.

"Exactly," Chloe replied. "Seth is so much more you."

Riley thought it over. After everything that had happened, a date with no strangeness seemed like it might be exactly what she needed. The truth was, Riley just wanted to relax and have a good time. Maybe Seth *was* the answer.

"Okay. Maybe it will work," Riley said with a small smile.

"Yea!" Chloe cheered. She wrapped Riley in a hug. "You won't regret it, I promise."

Riley took a deep breath. She liked Seth. He seemed like a nice guy. And he was a poet and a surfer and a basketball player. He was no Charlie, but maybe Chloe was right. Maybe that was a good thing.

Here goes nothing, Riley thought. Then she put on her brightest smile and walked back to the table. Okay, Cupid, she thought. Zing away!

"Your eighth-grade teacher really said one of your poems sounded like the back of a cereal box?" Riley asked.

"Yeah. And now I'm a published poet. So if anyone ever says your poetry is bad, don't take it to heart," Seth said with a laugh.

Riley smiled and leaned back in her chair. She and Seth had been talking and munching on a superlarge order of French fries for half an hour. She had to admit she was having a good time. Seth was funny, he knew everything there was to know about surfing, and he shared her taste in music down to the last CD. They hadn't argued once. He was totally unCharlie.

"Oh, hey. Cool bracelet," Seth said as Riley reached for a fry.

Riley looked down at her wrist. She was wearing the beaded bracelet Charlie had given her after the trivia contest. Just looking at it made her heart hurt. He had been so sweet that night, apologizing and bringing her the thoughtful gift. How had everything changed so quickly?

"Can I see it?" Seth asked.

"Sure," Riley said. She held out her arm so he could take a better look at the bracelet.

"My sister would love this," Seth said. "Where did you get it?"

"Oh . . . it came from this music store called Fracture," Riley said, her heart sinking lower with every minute.

What was she doing here? If she were really over Charlie, just thinking about him wouldn't make her feel this awful. And if she really liked Seth as more than a friend, she wouldn't be sitting here thinking about Charlie.

I still like him, Riley realized. And I can't date other people if I still like Charlie. As for Seth . . . he was a good guy, and she didn't want to lead him on.

"Seth, listen," Riley said as Seth held her hand, twisting it slightly so that the turquoise beads on her bracelet caught the light. "I have to tell you something."

At that moment the side door to the Beach House opened, distracting Riley. She looked up, and her breath caught in her throat. Charlie was standing there, but he didn't look anything like himself. He was wearing a red Billabong T-shirt and red and orange board shorts. He had Tevas on his feet and a shell bracelet around his wrist.

He looked just like every other guy in the *Teen Scene* Beach House. He blended right in.

All at once, Riley realized what he was doing. Charlie had dressed like that in order to fit in with her and her friends—to fit in with the kids at the Beach House. Just like Chloe had dressed up as a punk to go to Fracture.

Riley's heart warmed and felt as if it were swelling three sizes. She didn't want Charlie to change. She liked him just as he was. But she completely appreciated what he was trying to do. He had dressed in a way he hated just to try to win her back. He still liked her, and he was making an effort for her. It was the sweetest thing anyone had ever done for her.

Riley was about to stand up and excuse herself when she saw Charlie's eyes light on her. He started to smile, but then his gaze flicked to her hand—the hand Seth was still holding.

Instantly Charlie's face fell, taking Riley's heart with it. She knew what he was thinking. She had just broken up with him last night, and here she was holding hands with another guy. He'd come to make up with her and found her out on a date.

"Charlie!" Riley shouted as he turned to go. "Sorry, Seth," she said quickly. "I'll be back."

She followed Charlie out a side door and found him stalking across the sand.

"Charlie! Wait!" Riley called.

Charlie stopped but didn't turn around. Riley rushed up to him and stood in front of him.

"What are you doing here?" Riley asked. It was the first thing that popped into her head.

"I came to see you, but obviously I'm too late," Charlie said. His face was like stone.

"Charlie, no. You're not too late," Riley told him. He

93

shot her a look of disbelief, so she kept talking. "I mean, maybe that's not what it looked like—"

"It looked like you move on pretty fast," Charlie said, his voice thick with hurt. "Forget it, Riley. I never should have come here. Have fun with your new boyfriend."

With that, he turned and walked away. Riley stood still, watching him go. She felt as if her heart were breaking in two.

# chapter
## twelve

Chloe saw Charlie walk into the Beach House. She saw Riley's face brighten, then fall. She saw her sister chase after Charlie when he left, a panicked look on her face. The whole scene made Chloe realize something she hadn't realized before.

Riley really liked Charlie. A lot. And from the look on Charlie's face, he was totally in love with Riley.

Suddenly Chloe realized she had messed up big-time. Whatever their differences, Charlie and Riley belonged together. If they liked each other that much, they could find a way to make it work.

Chloe followed Charlie and Riley out the side door, hoping to make things right. The second Chloe opened the door, she saw Riley walking back toward the Beach House. Her shoulders were slumped, and she was paler than any Southern California girl should be.

"What happened?" Chloe asked, running to her sister's side.

"He thinks I like Seth," Riley said, blinking back tears. "I didn't know what to say."

"Well, maybe I do," Chloe said, rushing past her.

"Chloe, don't!" Riley called after her.

But Chloe ignored her. This was all her fault, and she would fix it if she could. All she really wanted was for her sister to be happy.

Chloe jogged around the side of the Beach House and saw a crowd of fans lined up by the back door. The bouncers were having a hard time controlling them as they jostled for space near the edge of the pathway. Chloe suddenly remembered that Nariah was supposed to make another appearance at the Beach House that day. This crowd must be waiting for autographs.

Of course, the crowd made it harder to spot Charlie. Finally she saw him on the other side of the group, making his way toward the boardwalk. Chloe took off at a run.

"Charlie!" she called as she caught up to him.

He paused and turned around. "If Riley sent you—"

"She didn't," Chloe said, out of breath. "Charlie, this is all my fault. You have to believe me. I set Riley up on that date."

"Maybe, but did you tell her to hold the guy's hand?" Charlie asked.

"No, but—"

"Listen, Chloe, I appreciate what you're trying to do, but I really can't talk about this anymore," Charlie said.

Chloe could see the hurt in his eyes, and she felt more guilty than ever.

"I have to go," Charlie said. He turned and walked up the steps to the boardwalk.

Just as Chloe was about to call out to him and try one more time, the crowd behind her let out a deafening scream. Charlie never would have heard her anyway.

Frustrated, Chloe turned and headed back down the sand. Nariah's limo was just pulling up, and all the fans were straining at the ropes. A few girls thrust pens and CDs toward Nariah as she stepped from the limousine.

Chloe took a detour around the back of the limo so as not to get caught up in the crazed crowd. Nariah paused to sign a few autographs and pose for some pictures. Meanwhile some woman who always seemed to be with Nariah started handing out pink and black tour T-shirts. Chloe barely even glanced at the pop star. She was too distracted by her thoughts of Riley and Charlie to care what Nariah was wearing today.

"Don't forget, everyone! Nariah's giving a concert at the arena tomorrow," the woman with the T-shirts called out. "If you don't have your tickets yet, you can win them from 103.7 Pop Rock!"

Chloe nodded to Barty, the bouncer at the side door who knew all the regulars. He stepped aside, and she was about to walk in when she heard a guy's voice shout Nariah's name.

Chloe looked up, and for a split second she could

have sworn she saw the flash of a dragon tattoo in the crowd. And was that Frodo with his crazy hair over there, diving toward the superstar?

Squinting, Chloe tried to get a better look, but she'd left her sunglasses in her bag, and the sun was blinding. The glare was playing tricks with her eyes, she decided. There was no way Jesse and Frodo were waiting for Nariah's autograph. She just had Charlie-related things on the brain.

Chloe walked into the Beach House and found Riley sitting at the snack bar with Lennon.

"Hey. Are you okay?" Chloe asked her sister.

"I will be," Riley said. "For now I just want to go home."

"Whatever you want," Chloe said.

"I'll walk you guys home," Lennon offered.

"Thanks," Chloe said. "Where's Seth?"

"I explained everything to him," Riley replied. "He was really cool about it, but he didn't want to stick around."

Chloe felt her heart squeeze. Somehow she'd managed to hurt Riley, Charlie, *and* Seth. She should not be allowed out of the house anymore.

"Let's get out of here," she said, wrapping an arm around Riley. Home sounded like the best place for both of them.

"I just feel so horrible every time I think of the look on Charlie's face," Riley said. She was lying on her bed doing her ceiling stare again. Chloe paced back and forth across the room, her mind in hyper-drive.

"We have to figure out a way to get him to listen to you. But how?" Chloe said.

"Hey, I have a question," Riley said, lifting herself up onto her elbows. "I thought there was something about Charlie you didn't like. Why do you suddenly want us together so badly?"

"I was wrong, okay? I can admit when I'm wrong," Chloe said.

"No, you can't," Riley replied.

"Okay, usually that's true. But this time I can," Chloe said. "Today I realized that you guys really like each other, and that's really all that matters."

"Well, what am I supposed to do? We both tried to talk to him, and he wouldn't listen," Riley pointed out.

"I've got it!" Chloe announced, sitting down on Riley's bed. Her eyes sparkled with excitement as she drew one leg up underneath her. "You need a grand romantic gesture!"

"What?" Riley sat up straight. "And why? I didn't do anything wrong!"

"I know, I know," Chloe said. "But think about it. What if it had been you? What if you had gone to one of his seedy little hangouts all dressed up like a skate chick to try to win him back, and then you found him holding some punk princess's hand?"

Riley thought that over for a moment. "You're right.

He's not going to listen to me until I do something to get his attention."

"Something big," Chloe said.

"Something monster-big," Riley added. "But what?"

"I don't know. But we have to figure it out, and we have to figure it out within the next twenty-four hours," Chloe said.

"Why? What happens after twenty-four hours?" Riley asked.

"Right now Charlie's hurt and confused," Chloe said. "But after a full day passes, he'll progress into the angry phase. You know what happens in the angry phase."

"He'll go out with other girls just to get back at me?" Riley guessed. They had read the same magazine article about this just last month.

"Exactly," Chloe said. "It's a classic boy strategy."

"We need to think," Riley said. "We need to think hard."

"I'll get the brain food," Chloe said, heading for the fridge. Some frozen yogurt was definitely called for. She was going to help Riley win Charlie back even if it killed her. It was the least she could do.

"Nothing! I've got nothing!" Riley cried.

"We're running out of time," Chloe said.

"I know! Stop with the pressure!" Riley said. She held out her hand, which was shaking like a leaf. "I think that last frappuccino was a bad idea."

"Well, you were falling asleep on me," Chloe reminded her.

They were leaning against the bamboo fence of the Beach House, brainstorming while the party raged all around them. After half a night of throwing out bad ideas—candygrams, flowers, skywriting—Chloe and Riley had gone to bed well after midnight and had woken up early. Still they had nothing. And the crucial twenty-four-hour deadline was ticking ever closer.

"Is this twenty-four-hour thing a strict rule?" Riley asked, feeling desperate.

"Give or take a few hours," Chloe said soberly.

"Okay, I need a bottle of water," Riley said. "I have to cleanse my system."

"I'll be here, thinking of more bad ideas!" Chloe called after her as Riley walked to the snack bar.

"One water, please," Riley told the guy behind the counter. She sighed and put her head in her hands. How could she feel so exhausted and so wired at the same time?

**[Riley: Mental note. Caffeine bad. Scary bad.]**

The snack-bar guy handed Riley a bottle of water and a red flier.

"What's this?" Riley asked.

"Some guy asked me to hand these out today," the guy replied. "Sounds like it could be pretty cool."

Riley looked down at the flier and her eyes widened.

Her pulse pounded even faster, which seemed impossible. The flier advertised Open Mike Night at Fracture. It was happening that very night!

Apparently Charlie and his dad had liked her last idea, and they were going with it. The thought made Riley psyched and sad at the same time. She had imagined hanging with Charlie on the Open Mike night, watching all the acts together. Now Charlie was going to be enjoying the show without her. And maybe even with some other girl.

Riley started back across the Beach House toward Chloe, staring at the flier.

"'All acts are welcome,'" she read aloud from the bottom of the page.

And then she stopped dead in her tracks. Some guy slammed into her from behind, surprised at her sudden stop.

"Hey! Bad party etiquette!" he griped.

"Sorry!" Riley said.

But she didn't care about her party etiquette. She had it! She'd finally figured it out. The perfect way to get Charlie to sit up and listen. She ran the rest of the way to her sister.

Chloe's face brightened the moment she saw Riley. "You've got it?" she asked.

Riley took a deep breath. "It's risky," she said. "But I've definitely got it."

# chapter
## thirteen

"I like these girls," Larry said, sitting back in his chair on Thursday night at Fracture. A duet was performing a slow song, and everyone in the audience was completely into it. "What do they call themselves?" Larry asked.

"Two Girls with Guitars," Lennon said.

"I know they're two girls with guitars, but what do they call themselves?" Larry asked again.

"Two Girls with Guitars," Chloe told him.

"Whatever. If you guys don't want to tell me, don't tell me." Larry turned back to the stage, frustrated.

Riley was too busy being nervous to take part in deconfusing Larry. Sometimes that was impossible anyway. She sat a few inches back from the table, reading and rereading the page in her lap. She hadn't seen Charlie yet, but he had to be here. This whole thing was pointless if he wasn't here.

"Are you ready?" Chloe asked as the duet finished their song.

"Where's Charlie?" Riley whispered.

"His father said he would find him before you went on," Chloe replied. "Don't worry."

Riley's heart beat double-time in her chest as the last guitar strains faded away. The room burst into applause, and Two Girls with Guitars took a bow. Then Charlie's father walked up onto the stage.

"Can you do this?" Chloe asked, worried.

"I think so," Riley replied. She wiped her sweaty palms on her jeans.

"Thank you, Two Girls with Guitars!" Charlie's father said.

"Sheesh! Even *he* doesn't know their names!" Larry said, throwing up his hands. Lennon hung his head.

"Next up we have Riley Carlson reciting her own poetry," Charlie's father announced.

There was a smattering of applause as Riley stood.

"Break a leg!" Chloe gave her sister's hand an encouraging squeeze.

"Thanks," Riley said. She knew she looked nervous.

[Riley: Make that terrified. Have you ever gone for one of those all-or-nothing deals? Basically it feels as if your whole life is on the line. You're either going to make everything a whole lot better—or a whole lot worse.]

She wound her way around the tables and chairs. It seemed as if the walk to the stage took forever. When she stood behind the mike, she looked at the two tables where Chloe, Lennon, Larry, Amanda, Quinn, and Tara were sitting. At least she had a cheering section.

She saw Charlie's dad disappear through a door in the back marked STORAGE.

"This poem is called 'Opposites Attract,'" Riley said into the microphone.

At that moment Charlie stepped out from the storeroom. He leaned back against the doorjamb, crossed his arms over his chest, and watched her. He looked as if he wasn't quite sure what to make of the fact that Riley was standing on the stage at his father's store.

Riley cleared her throat, looked down at the page, then realized she didn't need to. After all the times she had read it over, she had the poem memorized.

*"You are the night, I am the day.*
*You are the mountains, I am the sea.*
*You like things spicy, I like them sweet.*
*You like the boardwalk, I like the beach.*
*This is who we are.*
*We're different, it's true,*
*But I know what I like.*
*I like me with you."*

Riley looked Charlie directly in the eye as she finished her poem. She wanted to make sure there was no doubt in his mind that it was about him. There was a moment of silence after Riley finished her poem, and then the room burst into applause. Riley quickly stepped off the stage and walked over to Charlie. He shoved his hands into the pockets of his jeans and stood up straight. For a long moment he didn't say a thing.

"That took a lot of guts," he finally said.

"I feel like I left them onstage somewhere," Riley admitted, holding a hand over her stomach, which was clenched with nerves.

"That was for me?" Charlie asked.

"Of course it was for you," Riley said. "You ran off so fast yesterday, I never had a chance to explain. Seth was just admiring my bracelet, that's all."

"I had no right to be mad anyway," Charlie said. "I heard what Lily said to you at her party. After that I wouldn't blame you for going out with other guys."

"But I don't want to go out with other guys," Riley said. "I want to go out with you."

Charlie grinned. "Yeah?"

"Yeah," Riley said.

"What about Lily?" Charlie asked.

"Eh. I can take her," Riley joked.

"And Jesse and Frodo?" Charlie asked.

"I can take them, too," Riley said. "I'm tougher than I look."

Charlie laughed, reached out, and pulled her into a hug. "So we're cool?" he asked.

"We're cool," Riley said with a nod. "I mean, just because we don't like all the same things, that doesn't mean we can't date, right?"

"Well, actually, I have to tell you, I really liked that CD you gave me," Charlie said quietly. "Don't tell anyone, but I was dancing to it in my room the other day."

"The Rocketship CD? I knew it!" Riley cried. "I knew you'd love them!"

"Keep it down!" Charlie said, looking around nervously. "You don't want to trash my rep as a punk, do you?"

"Oh, no. Wouldn't want to do that," Riley said sarcastically.

"What about you?" Charlie asked. "Did you like the Purple Slice CD?"

"Um . . . well . . . no," Riley said, wincing.

"What? You're kidding! That's their best album!" Charlie said.

"If you say so," Riley said with a laugh. "They're just so . . . angry. I'm more of a bright-side person myself."

"Yeah. That's one of the things I like about you," Charlie said. He reached out and clasped her hand in his.

"What else do you like about me?" Riley teased.

"Um, can I have some time to think on that one?" Charlie said, his eyes sparkling.

Riley whacked him in the chest, and then Charlie leaned down and kissed her quickly on the lips. It was so fast, it nearly took Riley off her feet.

"I liked *that*," Charlie said, squeezing her hand gently.

"Yeah," Riley said with a smile. "Me, too."

Chloe watched Riley and Charlie kiss and practically had to sit on her hands to keep from clapping. It was all so movie-perfect: the poem, the dramatic make-up talk, the kiss. Maybe it had been good for Riley and Charlie to break up just so that they could *make* up with a moment like that.

"Feeling better?" Lennon asked her.

"A hundred percent," Chloe assured him. She glanced around the store. "You know, this place isn't so bad after all," she said happily. Tonight she had worn a regular Chloe outfit—denim miniskirt, red halter top, non-psycho makeup—and she hadn't noticed a single person staring at her. Maybe that was because she no longer cared if she fit in. She was fine just as she was.

"Well, I'm impressed that you came here for Riley tonight after telling me you never wanted to step foot in this troll hole again," Lennon said with a smile.

"I did not call it a troll hole," Chloe countered.

"Those were your exact words," Lennon reminded her.

Chloe sighed. "Do you have to remember everything I say?"

"You love it," Lennon said, holding her hand.

"Okay, I kind of do."

As Chloe glanced toward the stage, where a guy was

playing the bongos and rapping about L.A. smog, something at the back of the room caught her eye. Jesse and Frodo were slipping into the store through the back door and sidling along the wall. They looked guilty. Something was definitely up.

Then Frodo turned slightly to say something to Jesse and Chloe saw a flash of pink under his jacket.

Chloe recognized that pink instantly. But it couldn't be, could it?

The bongo rap guy finished his performance, and everyone applauded politely. Chloe saw Frodo and Jesse heading for the bathroom, and she jumped up. It was just too perfect an opportunity. She couldn't pass it up.

"Where are you going?" Lennon yelled after her as she bolted for the stage.

"For revenge!" Chloe responded.

She grabbed the microphone the second the bongo rapper replaced it on the stand.

"Attention, everyone!" Chloe called out as she made her way to the back of the room and grabbed Jesse's arm. "What's the rush, guys?" she asked, which made Frodo stop, too. Chloe could feel everyone in Fracture turning to her and her two captives.

"I have a question for the room!" Chloe said. "Are these two guys: A) punks or B) phonies?"

Chloe looked at Frodo and Jesse, who had lost all color in their faces. Charlie's father turned the spotlight on them, and they blinked against the glare.

"It's a little warm in here, guys," Chloe said. "Why don't you take off your jackets?"

Frodo immediately hugged his jacket to his body, while Jesse gave Chloe a look of death.

"No way," Jesse said.

"Why not?" Chloe asked. "Got something to hide?"

"Take them off!" some guy yelled from across the room, causing a round of laughter. Everyone was watching now. Everyone was interested. Jesse and Frodo had no choice.

"Fine," Jesse said.

He looked at Frodo, and together they yanked off their jackets. The entire place exploded with laughter. There they stood, Jesse with his dragon tattoo and Frodo with his multiple piercings, wearing pink and black Nariah T-shirts.

"Hey!" Frodo shouted, grabbing the microphone from Chloe. "It was a good concert!"

This just made everyone laugh even harder. Frodo ducked into the bathroom, followed quickly by Jesse. Chloe gave a little bow and returned the microphone to the stage. She glanced over at Charlie and Riley, who were hugging and laughing. Charlie flashed Chloe a thumbs-up, and Chloe waved back.

She let out a contented sigh as everyone applauded her performance. Forget Jonah Bayou and the *Teen Scene* Spring Break Beach House. This was, without a doubt, her favorite moment of spring break.